Ghost Frequencies

NewCon Press Novellas

Set 1: *(Cover art by Chris Moore)*
    The Iron Tactician – Alastair Reynolds
    At the Speed of Light – Simon Morden
    The Enclave – Anne Charnock
    The Memoirist – Neil Williamson

Set 2: *(Cover art by Vincent Sammy)*
    Sherlock Holmes: Case of the Bedevilled Poet – Simon Clark
    Cottingley – Alison Littlewood
    The Body in the Woods – Sarah Lotz
    The Wind – Jay Caselberg

Set 3: The Martian Quartet *(Cover art by Jim Burns)*
    The Martian Job – Jaine Fenn
    Sherlock Holmes: The Martian Simulacra – Eric Brown
    Phosphorous: A Winterstrike Story – Liz Williams
    The Greatest Story Ever Told – Una McCormack

Set 3: Strange Tales *(Cover art by Ben Baldwin)*
    Ghost Frequencies – Gary Gibson
    The Lake Boy – Adam Roberts
    Matryoshka – Ricardo Pinto
    The Land of Somewhere Safe – Hal Duncan

Ghost Frequencies

Gary Gibson

NewCon Press
England

First published in the UK by NewCon Press
41 Wheatsheaf Road, Alconbury Weston, Cambs, PE28 4LF
June 2018

NCP 156 (limited edition hardback)
NCP 157 (softback)

10 9 8 7 6 5 4 3 2 1

ISBN:

978-1-910935-79-8 (hardback)
978-1-910935-80-4 (softback)

Cover art by Ben Baldwin
Cover layout by Ian Whates

Minor Editorial meddling by Ian Whates
Book layout by Storm Constantine

Prologue

She woke in the night, her skin clammy despite the warm summer breeze coming through the half-open window. She tried to move, to reach for the lamp by her bed, but her muscles remained locked in place. Night-terrors, the doctors called it – a fugue state somewhere between sleep and waking, as if giving it a name made the experience any less dreadful. They insisted on giving her endless pills, but they were useless. Every now and then she took the accumulated bottles and flushed their contents down the toilet.

She felt the presence. Imagined, rather than saw, a girl half-hidden in the shadows past her bed. She pictured hair that was stringy and unkempt.

Clara?

She tried to say the name, but her tongue remained as still as if it were locked inside her mouth. *Please*, she tried to say, willing her body to respond. *You're hurting me. Please...*

All of a sudden, she felt control return to her limbs. She jerked upwards with a lurch, an iron vice squeezing her heart, her breath fast and panicked.

She looked around, but there was nobody there. No one who could be seen, at least.

'Clara?' she managed to say. 'What is it?'

A whisper seeped up the stairwell, dense with static and just on the edge of audibility – a woman's voice. *Not Clara. You.*

Not Clara. That meant…the *other*, the one whose name she could never bring herself to say.

She clutched her nightgown close around her neck, catching sight of her shadowed reflection in the mirror atop her dressing-table. For a moment, she barely recognised the woman peering back at her – old beyond her years, her face lined like that of someone twenty years her senior.

A wren trilled its dawn-song. She swung narrow feet onto cold floorboards and lifted a cheap dressing-gown down from its hook before pushing her feet into slippers. She went downstairs to her cramped kitchen, the transistor radio next to the microwave hissing with static as it did every hour of every day.

Once, when her boiler had failed and workmen came to install a replacement, she had unplugged the radio for the first time in years, pushing it to the back of a cupboard. She still remembered her horror when the workmen had found the radio and turned it to some music station while they went about their trade. She remembered their expressions of perplexed amusement as she quickly unplugged it again before running upstairs with it. It had taken her weeks to rediscover the precise spot on the dial where the voices were strongest.

And so it had been for many years, bar the occasional power outage.

It's almost time, the same voice whispered from out of the static. *We're waiting for you.*

She stared at it, her thin gown clutched close around her neck. 'No,' she said, her face stricken with terror. 'I can't. I…can't.'

She will bring you a gift, without knowing it.

'Who will?' she asked, more weary than scared now. 'Bring me what?'

You must come back.

She stood there, listening to the dull roar of the radio, but heard nothing more.

You must have patience, Arthur Melville had once told her. *The spirits cannot be hurried. They have all eternity, and we do not.* He, at least, believed her. It had been his idea to write down everything the voices said.

She sighed, and pushed open the back door before stepping out into the small garden that lay behind her house, a red-brick semi that overlooked Wardenby. Rain pattered down onto the concrete and grass. When she looked across to the far side of the valley, she could see Ashford Hall, rising up where only a few years before had been nothing more than blackened ruins.

The voice hadn't said *where* she must go, but it hadn't needed to. Ashford Hall was the place she had long ago sworn never to return to. But the voice was insistent that one day she not only would, but *must* return there.

Even if it killed her.

She sighed, then stepped back inside, pulling open a drawer and retrieving her notebook and pen. She sat at the kitchen table and noted down the date and everything she remembered the voice had said to her while the first rays of morning chased shadows across the kitchen floor.

Wednesday July 1st 2020

'See what I mean?' asked Rajam, his upper body curled into a comma before the computer monitor. 'Noise in the signal.' He made a sucking sound with his teeth. 'I can't figure it out any more than you can.'

Susan, who had been standing behind his shoulder in order to study the histograms that crowded the screen, turned at the sound of the office door banging open. Andrew came stamping in, water dripping from the tip of his nose, his tweed jacket dark with rain. He dropped a shopping bag on a counter along with his car keys, then pulled a jar of instant coffee out of the shopping bag and switched on the kettle. 'You're here,' he said, nodding to Susan. 'I didn't see your car outside.'

'It's in for repairs.' She nodded at the computer. 'More bad news, I'm afraid.'

'More interference?' He came over, peering at Rajam's monitor.

'Same as before,' said Rajam, a faint rumble of techno issuing from the earbuds hanging around his shoulders. 'Regular radio and other communications with Beauty are fine, but as for anything spooky – nada.'

Andrew frowned. '"Spooky"?'

'Spooky action?' said Rajam with a roll of the eyes. 'At a distance?'

Andrew stared at him for a moment, then shook his head and turned to Susan. 'So just to be clear, we're officially no further on than we were two weeks ago?'

'I'm afraid not, no,' she admitted, hearing the defeat in her own voice. 'I'm open to suggestions.'

'Such as?' asked Andrew, stepping back over to the kettle and spooning coffee granules into a mug.

She shrugged. 'Witch doctor? Lucky charms? Because right now, I swear, I'm ready to try just about anything.'

'Well, first of all, don't panic,' said Andrew. The kettle clicked off and he made himself a coffee, carrying it over to the arched stone window to the left of Rajam's workstation. Outside, the wind stirred the trees lining the road to Wardenby, while farther away, ageing red brick homes stood along a road leading out of the valley. 'Is it the equipment, something in our measurements, or something else we haven't thought of that might be the source of our troubles?'

'Well,' said Rajam, looking sideways at Andrew, 'assuming for the moment everything's working the way it should, I don't see how our equipment could generate that much randomness without something affecting it from the outside. What if there's something that causes the quantum information to decohere before it reaches its destination?'

Andrew nodded, his gaze fixed on something outside. 'Like someone's reading our mail. But that still doesn't explain *how* they'd do it, even if there was someone else out there who *could* do it.'

'But we know there isn't,' Susan reminded him. She glanced towards the anteroom wherein the Beast resided. 'They'd have to have a quantum communications array matching ours, and apart from Beauty, there's no one else with a set-up like it.'

'There's always the Chinese,' suggested Andrew. 'Lord knows they're secretive enough.'

'I think that's a stretch,' said Susan. 'I keep thinking there's something right in front of us we're missing.' She thought for a moment. 'Maybe we need a fresh pair of eyes to take a look at the Beast.'

'I already checked everything thoroughly twice in the last fortnight,' said Rajam, a note of defensiveness creeping into his voice. 'Everything works the way it should.'

'Nobody's saying you've been anything but an enormous help to Susan, Rajam,' said Andrew, still peering out the window. 'By the way, there's a van parked outside that doesn't look like it belongs to the builders. Any idea whose it is?'

'Ask the security guard,' Susan suggested. 'He'd know.'

'I meant to do exactly that,' said Andrew, 'except I couldn't find him anywhere. I've a mind to make another complaint to the recruitment agency.'

'Now that I think of it, the front desk wasn't manned when I came in this morning either,' said Susan. 'I thought he'd gone off to use the toilet or something.'

Rajam tapped his keyboard and a mail program popped up over the histograms. 'I forgot to tell you,' he said. 'Apparently the day-shift hire quit. We got an email from the recruitment agency this morning.' He shrugged. 'Sorry. I guess he must have handed in his notice just last night.'

Susan stared at him. 'How many security guards has this place had since we started here? Three, in just two months? Or is it more?'

'Well, that's just bloody marvellous,' said Andrew, stepping back from the window. 'I suppose that means just anyone can come wandering in the building while people are working? Did they give a reason *why* he quit?'

''No,' said Rajam, glancing back at the screen, 'but his replacement gets here this afternoon. Oh – and I know why that van's here, but you're not going to like it.'

Andrew glowered at him. 'Why not?'

'Well, I saw some people unloading the van when I got here this morning, and I recognised one of them – a guy called Angus Moone. He got his Masters from Leith University about the same time I did. Anyway, we got talking, and it seems Christian Ashford hired them to carry out a study of Ashford Hall.'

Andrew looked perplexed. 'Christian was quite specific we'd have the place to ourselves for at least another couple of months. What *kind* of study?'

Christian, thought Susan. As if he and their billionaire benefactor were old friends and comrades, when in reality Andrew had never even met the man in the flesh.

'Apparently,' said Rajam, his mouth twisted up in an impish grin, 'they're ghost hunters.'

'Ghost –' Andrew's face flushed pink. 'I don't have time for this nonsense, Rajam.'

'It's the truth,' Rajam insisted in an aggrieved tone. He pulled out his mobile phone, his fingers moving rapidly across its screen. 'This guy is in charge of them,' he said, holding up the phone so they could see a still photograph of a grinning, portly man with a beard and a thick bush of hair that looked like it had been caught in a gale and then frozen in place. 'His name's Maxim Bernard. I remember him from when I was at Leith. They've got a whole department for perceptual research, which is a fancy way of saying the supernatural. Bernard's in charge of the department, and Angus is here to help him.'

The pink in Andrew's cheeks took on a darker hue. 'That's utterly ridiculous,' he spat. 'I'm sure they're nothing of the kind. Your friend was having you on.'

Rajam looked to Susan for help, then back at Andrew. 'I did actually *speak* with them,' he said. 'I'm not making it up. He didn't say specifically what they were here to look for, but he definitely used the words "haunted" and "Ashford Hall" in the same sentence.'

'*Ghost* hunters?' Susan asked him. 'Seriously?'

'Oh, for God's sake,' Andrew spluttered. 'Whatever they're doing here, the fact remains we were supposed to have this entire facility to ourselves until our work was completed.'

Susan raised an eyebrow. '*Our* work?'

'I meant your work, of course,' said Andrew, stepping towards the main door of the office, his mouth pinched up in an angry scowl. 'I'll go talk to them and sort out what's really going on. I'm sure there's a misunderstanding somewhere.'

'I'd rather you didn't –' Susan began to say, just as the door banged shut behind him. She listened for a moment to the sound of his shoes moving rapidly down the hallway.

'You're enjoying every second of this, aren't you?' she said, glaring at Rajam.

Rajam grinned broadly. 'Honestly, can you blame me?'

Susan hurried after Andrew, afraid he might make a scene. She stepped out of the office and saw him moving ahead of her in long, determined strides. She followed in his wake, passing unfinished and unoccupied labs with loose clusters of wiring still poking out of holes in their walls. She came to the top of the grand staircase -- a steep wash of cut steps that descended to the ground floor – in time to see Andrew hurrying down them.

At first glance, someone unaware of Ashford Hall's turbulent history might have thought the building to be centuries old, rather than a twenty-first century reconstruction in keeping with English Heritage's rigid specifications. The outside had been designed to resemble as closely as possible the original mansion built in the 1730s by Christian Ashford's ancestors, while his architects had rebuilt much of the interior based on old photographs from a pre-war collection. Yet it somehow *felt* as if it had stood undisturbed for centuries. Oak floorboards creaked beneath Susan's tennis shoes as if they had borne generations of feet, and dusty spider-webs clung to shadowy eaves that had only recently been rebuilt.

She hurried down the steps, seeing Andrew stride across the expanse of floor towards two men and a woman standing amidst a sea of crates and boxes. One of the men was in his mid-twenties, about Rajam's age – Angus Moone, presumably. The woman was older, perhaps in her thirties, with a short, brushy haircut above loose jeans and a sweatshirt. The second man was clearly Maxim Bernard.

'My name's Wrigley,' said Andrew, striding towards them. The woman glanced at Susan as she came hurtling up behind Andrew. 'Doctor Andrew Wrigley.' He turned to Bernard and extended his hand. 'You must be Maxim?'

'Ah!' Bernard replied with gusto, pumping Wrigley's hand up and down. 'Mr Ashford told me a research project was already up and running here. All very hush-hush, I gather.'

'Doctor Susan MacDonald,' Susan said quickly, moving to

shake Bernard's hand as well. 'Andrew's my project funding manager.'

'I apologise for being blunt,' Andrew broke in before Susan could say anything more, 'but I wondered if perhaps there's been some mistake? Chr –' He paused and cleared his throat. '*Mr* Ashford informed me we'd have the building to ourselves until at least the end of August. That's two months away.'

Susan saw something shift in Bernard's eyes. 'I don't see why –'

'Our work is of a commercially sensitive nature,' Andrew continued before Bernard could finish speaking. 'There's a risk that potential competitors might try and beat us to the punch if they got wind of what we're developing.' He smiled tightly. 'You can see why it's better if we have sufficient privacy to finish our work without risk of compromise.'

He glanced at Susan as he said this, and pretended he didn't see the hard glare on her face.

'Metka, Angus,' said Bernard, 'if you would be so kind as to start moving everything upstairs? We're in the West Wing, second floor. I'll be right up.'

His assistants got to work moving the crates over to the newly-installed elevator beneath the grand staircase, next to a door leading to the South Wing and the gardens.

'Mr Ashford mentioned you were working on some kind of prototype,' said Bernard, turning to Susan. 'I'm afraid he's already apprised me of the basic outlines of your work, although much of it went over my head. He wouldn't have shared that information if he wasn't already assured of my ability to maintain a professional confidence.'

Andrew made a pained sound.

'We signed NDA's,' Susan said to Bernard. 'I'm afraid we're really not allowed to talk about it to anyone.'

'Oh! Well, perhaps Mr Ashford spoke out of turn,' said Bernard, 'although it's clearly a matter of considerable enthusiasm to him.' He turned back to Andrew, whose face was full of stricken horror. 'I promise we'll be as quiet and unobtrusive as the proverbial church mouse, Doctor Wrigley,' he added, touching a finger to his lips.

'If you don't mind my asking,' said Susan, 'what is it that Ashford's brought you here for, exactly?'

'Please,' said Andrew, 'tell me you're not bloody ghost hunters!' He laughed unconvincingly.

Bernard nodded slowly. 'I think I'm beginning to understand the problem here. The preferred term is "parapsychologists." Perhaps you should take up the matter with Mr Ashford and discuss it with him directly?'

'If you could hold off on getting started until I speak to him,' said Andrew, 'I'd be enormously grateful.'

Bernard's eyes narrowed slightly. 'I think it's best we get started as soon as –'

'I beg to differ,' Andrew snapped. 'I –'

'I think Doctor Wrigley is just concerned that Mr Ashford didn't give us advance warning of your arrival,' Susan said quickly.

'I'll give him a call myself,' said Bernard, his gaze marginally less avuncular now. 'That should help straighten things out.'

Andrew brushed an invisible hair from his jacket, suddenly ill at ease. 'That's very kind of you, Mister Bernard.'

'*Professor* Bernard,' the other man corrected him. 'And the pleasure's all mine.'

Once they had made their way back up to the second floor, Andrew turned to Susan. 'I didn't handle that very well, did I?'

'I'd rather you didn't speak on my behalf,' said Susan, fighting down her anger. 'I'm happy for you to project-manage my work, but what's going to happen once other research teams turn up here? Are you going to scream and shout at *them*?'

He stared at her, his expression incredulous. 'They're *ghost hunters*. Surely you, of all people, understand how important reputation is in any field. We can't be seen to be associated with them in any way, not even by proximity.'

'I don't care,' said Susan, her expression increasingly frosty. 'What Ashford does with his money is his business. If you have a problem with it, ask him yourself. You said you were going to.'

Andrew nodded, apparently oblivious to her anger. 'I certainly intend to.' He shook his head and chuckled. 'My God, how does Ashford square superstitious nonsense like that with building a state-of-the-art research centre?'

Thursday July 2nd 2020

'I promise you that Professor Bernard and his team will be entirely discreet,' said Ashford, looking rumpled but tanned on the screen of Andrew's laptop the next day. 'They won't get in your way. You can be assured of that.'

It was early morning in California and four in the afternoon in Britain. Andrew had chased Rajam into the furthest corner of the office, then inveigled Susan into sitting beside him when Ashford came online. She was, after all, as he reminded her for the umpteenth time, the reason they were all there.

'But *why*?' demanded Andrew, sounding more like a schoolboy whose school trip had been cancelled than a former Senior Researcher at CERN.

Ashford leaned forward, and Susan saw he was sitting on a verandah. Sunlight glinted from a sun-kissed shore that seemed impossibly exotic compared to rain-lashed England. 'Professor Bernard spends more time debunking the paranormal than anything else. It's the summer break, Andrew – he has conferences to attend, and university work to prepare for. This is the only time he has available. It has to be now.'

'With the greatest respect,' said Andrew, 'if anyone else in the scientific community got wind of supernatural investigators wandering around what's meant to be a modern scientific research centre, it'd harm the chances of our project being taken seriously. It would be-' he paused, searching for the right word '-*tainted*.'

'If I worried what other people thought of me, Andrew,' said Ashford, 'I'd never have achieved one damn thing in life. Results count, nothing else. If your quantum communications array does what we're all hoping it can do, governments and telecommunications corporations all around the world will be too busy handing us enormous amounts of money to care less about whatever Professor Bernard finds or doesn't find. In fact, I guarantee you Maxim isn't going to find squat. That's why he's there – to prove there *aren't* any ghosts.'

'But how does that make sense?' asked Susan. 'Why hire someone to investigate a haunted house if you don't believe it's haunted?'

Ashford grinned. 'Because Ashford Hall has been a magnet for wackos for years, and I want all that bullshit put to rest. There's been whole books written about the place and the ghost that's supposed to haunt it. Some kook even held a séance there when it was still a pile of ruins.' He chuckled to himself. 'I want Ashford Hall to be a centre for serious scientific research just as much as you do, Andrew. And if it means I have to hire Maxim to put a stop to all that crap, then so be it.'

'Well,' said Andrew, only partly mollified, 'I suppose that's something. But just to be clear, Mr Ashford, I'd still rather they weren't here at all.'

Susan darted Andrew an angry look as if to say, *what do you mean you'd* rather?

Ashford must have seen Susan's expression, because his gaze shifted towards her. 'And how about you, Doctor MacDonald? Do you share Andrew's feelings on the matter?'

'My feeling is that it's none of my business,' she said, 'as long as they don't interfere with our ability to do our work. And I don't see any reason to think they would.'

Ashford turned back to Andrew. 'So if Susan feels that way, then there's really no problem, is there?'

Andrew's jaw worked as if he was eating something

spectacularly sour. 'Perhaps not,' he said in a slightly strangled voice.

'Of course,' said Ashford, looking back at Susan, 'all of this would be moot if you'd produced any tangible results.' He smiled at her suddenly frozen expression. 'I *have* been keeping tabs on your daily updates, you know.'

'We're considering the possibility our experiment is suffering from some kind of localised interference,' she managed to say.

'Any idea what that might be?'

'I don't know,' Susan admitted, hating the finality of the words. 'Not yet. We're working on it, obviously.'

Ashford stared past his computer's lens for what felt like a very long time. 'All right,' he said at last. 'Cards on the table. Business-wise, I'm taking a hit right now, and while my pockets are deep, they aren't bottomless.'

'Does that mean you aren't going to finish building Ashford Hall?' asked Andrew.

'No, no,' said Ashford, 'that's all going ahead. In fact, the renovators are due to make a last-minute push to get everything finished as soon as possible. No, I'm just reminding you that there's only so long I can keep pouring money into your research without solid, reproducible results.'

'Then... How long do we have?' asked Susan.

'Let's see where we are a week from now,' said Ashford. He smiled broadly. 'Look, I'm still really excited about the work you're doing. And even if you don't achieve everything you hoped to, there's at least a couple of things in there my guys say could be worked into solid patents.' His hand reached out towards them. 'Sayonara.'

Ashford disappeared from the screen and Andrew slammed the lid of his MacBook down. 'Arrogant prick,' he muttered.

'The other day you were acting like you were on first name terms.'

'Because he's made of money,' he replied tonelessly. 'Endless amounts of money. Yet he's as tight-fisted as the worst of them.'

'I don't know if I can figure this out in just a week,' she told him.

Andrew laughed hollowly. 'Starting to miss academia yet?'

'More than I expected,' she admitted. 'What did you make of that story of his, about Bernard being here to *disprove* a ghost? I don't get that.'

Andrew nodded. 'I admit it sounded fishy to me.'

'I know why,' said Rajam.

Susan glanced around to see him squeezed into a corner by a desk, tapping at his own laptop. 'Something you heard from your friend Angus?'

'Bernard's here because the security staff keep quitting,' Rajam explained. 'I met Angus at the Grey Lady for a pint last night and he told me all about it. Seems they were always hearing things moving around at night, or hearing disembodied voices. Apparently the agency that supplies them is having to recruit staff from further and further away from here, because nobody local's willing to come near the place.'

Andrew gave him a bug-eyed stare. 'Please tell me *you* don't believe in any of this nonsense.'

'Me?' Rajam made a snorting sound. 'Of course not. I haven't seen or heard a bloody thing.'

'In fairness,' said Andrew, 'you walk around in a haze of deafening House music. You wouldn't notice a 747 landing on top of us.'

'I haven't heard anything either, I must admit,' said Susan.

'Well of course you haven't,' said Andrew, giving her a perplexed look. 'Because there's nothing to bloody hear.'

Friday July 3rd 2020

'Whatever it is,' Rajam said the next morning, 'it's nothing to do with the Beast.' He nodded at his laptop. 'Right, Bethany?'

Rajam sat perched on a stool next to the Beast, a collection of custom-built and precision-engineered widgets, mirrors and lasers mounted on a low table in a dedicated room next to the office he shared with Susan and Andrew. He had wedged his laptop onto one corner of the table, and had been running a series of diagnostic tests since he'd arrived that morning. A window on his screen showed his opposite number, Bethany, in California. She was in charge of maintaining an identical experimental setup codenamed Beauty.

There was a delay of about a second before Bethany's reply. 'Everything reads fine, Doctor MacDonald,' she said to Susan, who sat on another stool next to Rajam's. 'I guess whatever the problem is, it's nothing to do with either Beauty or Beast.' She paused for a moment, then leaned closer to the lens before asking – 'Doctor MacDonald, have you heard anything about the Chinese?'

'Heard what?'

'Well... there's a rumour Xin Ping is putting together his own retrocausality experiment that sounds an awful lot like yours. I don't know if it's because they got wind of what we've been doing, or if they were already working on the same kind of thing.'

Susan fought the urge to swear out loud. 'I didn't know. But thanks for the heads-up, Bethany.'

Bethany smiled the cheery smile of someone who didn't have the weight of a multimillion dollar experiment resting on her shoulders. 'If there's anything else you think we should try...?'

Susan shook her head. 'Not that I can think of.' What a shame, she thought, that they didn't hand out Nobel prizes for groundbreaking experiments that *almost* worked.

'Maybe it's the ghost,' Rajam said to Susan with a grin. 'Maybe it's the one causing our transmissions to decohere.'

'Ghost?' asked Bethany with renewed interest. 'What ghost?'

'He's kidding,' Susan said quickly. 'Thanks for your help, Bethany.' She closed the lid of Rajam's computer and gave him a stern look.

'What?' Rajam demanded, looking hurt. 'I was only joking.'

'Try joking like that when Andrew's around.'

Rajam winced. '*Ouch.* All right, so what now?' He glanced at his watch. 'Apart from getting lunch, that is.'

'Well,' said Susan, 'if this is anything like the movies, I go home and despair until a last-minute breakthrough drops into my head and saves the day.'

'Nice idea,' said Rajam. 'Although the movies I watch have more kickboxing than conceptual breakthroughs.'

She stood, cuffing him lightly across the top of the head as she headed for the door. 'And that, Rajam, is why you can never get a date.'

She left Rajam to get on with reconstructing the array components he'd pulled apart during their investigation. She opened her own laptop, only to find the battery charge was close to zero. She dug around in her backpack, but couldn't find the power cord.

'Rajam,' she asked, looking back through the connecting door, 'do we have any power cables lying about? I think I left mine at home.'

'There's a spare in my car,' he said, putting a half-assembled component down. 'I'll get it.'

'No, it's fine,' she said. 'I could do with a walk. Give me your keys and I'll go get it.'

She made her way back down the corridor to the top of the

grand staircase, where the South, West and East Wings converged. She was about to make her way downstairs when she heard a loud *bang* coming from down the South Wing corridor.

She paused, her hand on the balustrade, but heard nothing more. Most likely it was the builders continuing their renovation work. The South Wing was the last part of the building to be finished. Despite their best efforts, it wouldn't officially open until the autumn.

She found Rajam's spare cable in the boot of his car, then realised she couldn't see the builder's van. If they weren't here, then just who or what was making all the noise?

She went back inside, a prickle of uncertainty running up her spine as she looked up at the top of the staircase. Most likely one of the builders had gone off in the van to collect more supplies while the others got on with their work. Or possibly it was Bernard or one of the other parapsychologists, doing whatever it was they did.

Either of which was a perfectly reasonable explanation, yet the prickling in her skin only grew as she ascended the steps.

She heard another thump, like a sack of concrete being dropped somewhere down the South Wing corridor, then something that might have been a voice. She glanced back down at the reception desk, still unmanned despite the recruitment agency's promises. Well-organised thieves could have a field day in a place like Ashford Hall, with all the state-of-the-art equipment still sitting around in shrink-wrap and waiting to be installed – especially if they didn't know people were already working there.

She took a step down the corridor. 'Hello?' she called out, her voice echoing in the dusty silence.

Then she heard whistling and felt herself relax. It was probably Bernard or one of his assistants. Perhaps, she thought, this would be a good opportunity to say hello without Andrew present.

She made her way further down the corridor, passing more empty and unfinished labs and offices. A paint-stained ladder stood next to a wall, loops of fibre-optic cable as well as hammers and other tools lying next to it. She came to a balcony at the end, more stairs leading down to the lower floor and the gardens.

The whistling was coming from a door immediately to the left of the balcony, and it stopped when she stepped towards it.

'Hello?' she said again.

She looked inside the room, but there was no one there. She stared around, bewildered. A trick of the acoustics, she thought. New floorboards stood leaning against walls that were still scarred with graffiti from the days Ashford Hall had been a ruin. Plywood sheets had been laid over naked joists so that workmen could move around inside without putting their feet through the plaster beneath. She also saw a pair of shotgun mikes, mounted on angled boom poles in opposite corners.

She had stepped further into the room, balancing on one of the plywood sheets, when she heard a sharp, indrawn breath from just behind her shoulder...

She gasped and turned quickly enough that one of the plywood sheets slid out from under her feet. She lost her balance and fell onto all fours, her right foot slipping into a gap between two joists. Her shoe came loose, tumbling into the gap.

Shit. She stared around, her heart thundering in her chest. There was no one there.

And yet she'd *heard* something.

It's the wind, dummy, she told herself. *It finds its way inside old places like this.*

Except, she remembered, this wasn't really an old building at all. It was just built on the ruins of one.

She pushed one of the plywood boards aside until she could see where her shoe had fallen. As she reached down for it she noticed something glinting faintly in the shadows deep between the joists. It looked like a piece of jewellery, resting against an old and rotten joist just where it met one of the walls.

She wondered how long it had been lying there, waiting to be found. She pulled her shoe back on, then leaned down again, reaching for the trinket. It took an effort to snag it, half-hidden as it was behind a brick.

She squatted on the plywood, examining her newfound treasure: a simple silver bracelet of the kind you'd find being sold for a few pounds in a high-street jewellers. She felt strangely disappointed it hadn't turned out to be something more obviously valuable. She examined the bracelet more closely, finding it consisted of a slightly curved plate with a thin chain attached.

She stood back up and pushed the bracelet into her pocket to examine later.

'Find something?'

Susan stiffened, and turned to see the short-haired woman who had been with Professor Bernard watching her with some curiosity from the doorway.

'No,' Susan lied immediately, then wondered why she had.

The woman nodded. 'I thought perhaps you had,' she said. Her accent sounded Polish.

'Metka, isn't it?' asked Susan, making her way carefully across the plywood boards before extending a hand. 'We met the other day.'

Metka nodded. 'Doctor Wrigley seemed very upset.'

Susan allowed herself a small chuckle. 'He's really not that bad.'

Metka nodded at the joists. 'You were looking for something?'

Susan smiled sheepishly. 'I heard someone whistling. I came to see who it was and I slipped and lost my shoe. I thought it might be the builders, but...'

'Ah.' Metka nodded, then frowned. 'Builders are not here today. No one is here.'

'Well, no,' Susan said, a touch awkwardly. 'Obviously I realise that *now*.'

'Nor is there anyone to whistle,' Metka added. She regarded Susan thoughtfully, then rooted around in her pocket before withdrawing a handheld device like a mobile phone with six fat buttons beneath an LCD screen: an EMF meter.

'What are you doing?' Susan asked, coming up beside Metka to look at it.

'I'm checking for higher than expected levels of electromagnetic activity,' Metka replied. Her phrasing sounded uncertain, in the manner of one speaking a language they were not yet entirely comfortable with. She held the device up so Susan could clearly see rows of numbers on its screen rising rapidly before finally peaking. 'Quite a lot of EM activity, it seems.'

'They're installing a lot of equipment,' Susan pointed out.

'There's wiring everywhere. It's probably just that.'

Metka smiled, just very faintly. 'The South Wing is still very much under construction. The only electronic equipment here is ours,' she said, nodding at the tripod-mounted microphones.

'Please don't say it's ghosts,' said Susan, her voice flat.

Metka laughed good-naturedly. 'Most likely you're quite right.' She pocketed the meter and Susan followed her back out into the corridor, seeing several more shotgun mikes wrapped up in bin bags and leaning against a wall. A similar bundle of long boom sticks sat next to it.

'We have been placing equipment all around Halls for our study,' Metka explained. 'Listening devices, cameras, and various other pieces of equipment. If anyone sneezed, let alone whistled, we would know.'

'I should get going,' Susan said, feeling suddenly at a loss for anything else to say.

'Of course,' said Metka as Susan hurried away. 'See you around.'

Susan pushed her hand into the pocket of her jeans and felt the bracelet still there, and wondered why she felt so much like a thief.

Monday July 6th 2020

She ran into Metka again on the way out of Wardenby's one small Sainsbury's on the following Monday morning, three days after their encounter in the South Wing. It was Susan's turn to buy coffee and milk, plus the Hobnobs that appeared to form the primary component of Rajam's diet. She had shoved the shopping bag into her backpack before heading for the taxi rank, her car still being in for repairs.

'Susan!'

She turned around to see Metka get out of a battered Volkswagen Polo parked across from the post office. She waved to Susan before crossing the road to join her. 'You are on your way to work?'

'I am,' said Susan. 'You?'

'I was going to get some breakfast first. Why don't you join me?'

'Well...'

'There's a café I like,' said Metka. 'They have very good toasted sandwiches. You will join me, yes?' she enquired hopefully.

Susan guessed which café she meant. Her AirBnB came with free WiFi, but it was far from reliable, and the Karma Café at least had decent WiFi, even if there was barely room for half a dozen people to squeeze onto its tiny stools.

'Perhaps you're in a hurry,' said Metka, seeing her hesitation.

'No, not at all,' she replied. In truth, until they could figure out the problem with their experiment, there wasn't very much for her or Rajam to do.

'Good.' Metka beamed at her.

The Karma Café turned out to be empty at that time of the morning, apart from the owner, a slightly Goth-looking woman in her forties who, at that moment, was standing behind the counter with her iPad propped against a coffee jar. Susan ordered a black coffee with no sugar and felt obscurely pleased when Metka did the same. They both ordered toasted sandwiches.

'So,' said Metka, sipping her coffee when it arrived on the rickety table between them, 'how is your work going, if I may ask?'

Susan wondered how much she could say without seeming rude, then remembered the conversation with Professor Bernard and his revelation that Christian Ashford was all too forthcoming with the details of their work. 'You know we had to sign NDA's,' she began cautiously.

Metka nodded. 'We had to do the same.'

Susan looked at her in surprise. 'You did?'

'Mr Ashford said he wants to keep his affairs private. He doesn't want press to know we're at Ashford Hall. He believes it would bring negative publicity.'

Susan laughed hollowly and wondered what Andrew would make of that. 'Well then, he's shite at keeping secrets, let me tell you.'

'This is true,' Metka agreed. 'Unfortunately for him, one of the builders recognised Maxim and asked him if he was a ghost hunter. He had no choice but to say yes.'

'That sounds like a stroke of bad luck.'

'Not really,' said Metka. 'Besides, I don't believe in secrets. And Maxim has been on television talking about the supernatural, so it would hardly be surprising when someone recognises him.'

So much for NDAs, thought Susan. Their toasted sandwiches arrived, and the café-owner gave the both of them a curious look through kohl-rimmed eyes before retreating back behind her iPad.

Metka took a bite of her sandwich and grunted with pleasure.

'Don't take this the wrong way,' said Susan, lowering her voice slightly, 'but there's good reasons for us wanting to keep our work a secret. It's... kind of on the fringes.'

'Blue-sky research, yes?' asked Metka, crunching her way through her meal. 'The kind of thing for which it's hard to get funding unless you have a private billionaire investor.'

All of which was quite correct. 'I heard from Rajam – he's our research assistant – that Ashford hired you because our security staff keep quitting.'

'Rajam. I remember.' Metka nodded and drank her coffee. 'We're Ashford's final strategy before he brings in an exorcist.'

Susan felt her mouth slide open. 'Excuse me?'

'The official story,' said Metka, 'were the press to learn of our presence in Wardenby, is that we're there to disprove the existence of previously reported supernatural manifestations. But if we *did* discover evidence of manifestations, Ashford's intention is to employ an exorcist from California.'

'And Ashford told you this himself?'

'I heard it from Maxim, who heard it in turn from Ashford.'

'Should you really be telling me this?' asked Susan. 'If Ashford told you all this in confidence...'

'You're working in Ashford Hall,' Metka pointed out. 'You heard something where there was no one.'

'Well, yes,' Susan stammered, 'but –'

'It's evidence, regardless of what you think it is evidence *for*,' Metka continued. 'We cannot do our study without knowledge of activities elsewhere in Ashford Hall. If people like yourself see or hear something, we need to know. Secrecy would make the collection of data near to impossible. I'm telling you all this so that you understand.'

Susan looked at her with a troubled expression. In fairness, everything Metka said made perfect sense. 'So... does that mean you believe in ghosts yourself?'

Metka picked up one of the remaining crusts from her toasted sandwich and chewed on it thoughtfully, and Susan suddenly realised she had hardly touched her own. She picked it up and bit into it.

'I believe in that for which there is evidence,' said Metka. 'My background is in engineering.' She smiled at the look on Susan's face. 'You're surprised.'

'How on Earth does an engineer wind up hunting ghosts?'

'The same way Doctor Andrew Wrigley ended up involved with your own experiment,' Metka explained. 'Correct me if I'm wrong, but my understanding is that Wrigley has his own project he wishes to fund with Mr Ashford's help. But in order to get that funding, he must first project-manage your experiments.'

'No, you're quite right,' Susan told her. 'So does that mean you're here for more than just helping Professor Bernard?'

'Don't get me wrong – paranormal investigation is a great interest of mine, and I wished for a long time to work with Professor Bernard,' said Metka. 'But my training is in satellite communications systems. That requires an understanding of physics, although to be honest I'm not sure I really understood the details of your work any more than Maxim did.'

Susan shook her head. 'I wonder why the man even bothered having us sign NDA's.'

'I think he doesn't mind talk between groups that work for him,' Metka pointed out. 'People outside of Ashford Hall are presumably another matter.'

It occurred to Susan that if Metka's speciality was satellite communications systems, then it was entirely possible it would tie into her own research into new communications technologies. In that case, there could indeed be some value in getting to know Metka. 'All right,' she said. 'tell me what you *do* know about my work.'

'Something to do with boosting radio signals so can cross space without taking any time to do it?' Metka's mouth crinkled up in an embarrassed grin.

'That's pretty much the gist of it.'

'But *instantaneous* communications?' Metka chuckled quietly. 'How is such a thing even possible?'

'If you've studied physics, then you've surely heard of spooky action at a distance.'

'I know it means particles that can talk to each other no matter how far apart they are,' Metka agreed.

'Exactly,' said Susan. 'You start with a pair of entangled particles. Whatever changes you make to one are reflected in the other instantaneously, no matter if they're sitting right next to each other or separated by light-years. Einstein didn't like the idea because it implied faster-than-light communication.'

'It doesn't?'

'For complicated reasons, no, not really.'

'Then... How does one particle *know* what happens to the other?'

'Nobody knows,' Susan replied. 'It's probably down to some hidden variable we've not yet detected, but which in turn accounts for the detectable data. There are theories, of course.'

'Ah.' Metka leaned back with her coffee clutched in both hands. 'You're testing a theory at Ashford Hall?'

'More like a variation on someone else's theory,' she said. 'Someone came up with the idea that instead of information being carried across the intervening space between a particle and its twin, perhaps instead the first particle transmits its information *backwards* in time, to the point at which the two particles first became entangled. Then that information, because it's now contained within both particles, is carried forward in time until it's finally detected at its destination *in the same moment that it's sent*. That would overcome Einstein's objections.'

'This sounds like time travel,' said Metka, looking impressed. 'Surely such a thing is impossible?'

'No more impossible than two particles that can seemingly exchange information from one end of the universe to the other without the apparent passage of time,' said Susan. 'And yet they clearly do.'

'My God,' said Metka, looking delighted. 'You're building a *time machine*.'

'It is *not* a time machine,' Susan insisted, putting up both hands. She glanced over at the café-owner, who was trying very hard not to look like she was listening in to their conversation. 'It's just a communications device,' she continued, lowering her voice. 'Imagine you could control a rover on Mars with instantaneous two-way communication, instead of having to wait at least fifteen minutes for a radio signal to get there and another fifteen for a response to come back. You could drive it around the surface of Mars in real-time, with no delay.' And indeed part of the reason for Ashford's investment in her work lay in his hope of selling qubit transceivers to both the military as well as the civilian satellite industries.

''Ere,' said the café-owner, clearing her throat. 'Apologies if I'm interrupting, but you're from up at the Halls, right?'

Susan glanced at Metka, then nodded. 'We are. Why?'

The woman seemed to take this as an invitation to join them. 'My husband's mate's been working on the refurbishment,' she said, coming to stand by their table. She nodded at Metka. 'You're here about the ghost, right? You're working with the bloke from the telly.'

'*The* ghost?' asked Susan. It suddenly occurred to her despite the presence of Professor Bernard and his colleagues, she had no idea of the nature of Ashford Hall's apparitions.

'You know something about it?' Metka asked the café-owner.

A look of conspiratorial delight sped across the woman's face. 'I used to go up there when I was young, me and my mates.' She shook her head. 'Not anymore,' she said, before adding, in a loud stage whisper: 'I'm a touch psychic, you see.'

Susan opened her mouth to say something about that, but Metka shot her a silent warning and she closed her mouth again.

'You've seen it?' Metka asked her. 'The ghost?'

'Well, no.' The woman's face fell slightly. 'But I've *heard* it, back about the time that Ashford bloke was still dealing pills.'

'What?' Susan stared at the woman. 'Dealing pills...?'

Metka's attention remained fixed on the other woman. '*Christian* Ashford, yes?' she asked, and the woman nodded. 'I read his autobiography. He's come a very long way from being such a troublemaker when he was a young man.'

Susan looked from one to the other in utter stupefaction. 'I had no idea about this. Are you serious?'

'Well, I knew 'im back then,' said the café-owner. 'Posh bloke, old money, you know? His mum and dad died and left him a huge wad, but he couldn't get it until he was twenty-one.'

'And that's why he dealt pills?' asked Susan.

'He liked the rich life,' the woman agreed. 'Mostly hash, really – the pills were more of a sideline. Girls liked him because he flashed his money around. Then of course he had that run-in with the law before he got his act together and buggered off to the States.'

'I knew about the investing in Silicon Valley bit,' said Susan, 'but all this is news to me. I –'

'For God's sake, Samantha,' said a voice from over beside the café entrance. Susan turned to see a man in a dark suit standing there. Despite his words, he was smiling. 'Stop bothering the poor ladies with gossip.'

'I wasn't doing anything of the kind,' Samantha said indignantly.

The man shook his head at Susan and Metka. 'She tells everybody the same story about how Christian Ashford used to go riding around Wardenby on a motorbike scaring old ladies.' He leaned over the counter and hit a button on the till machine that made its cash drawer open. He dropped a couple of pound coins inside it, then grabbed a pair of plastic-wrapped sandwiches from a plate on the counter and dropped them into his suit pocket.

'I wish you wouldn't do that,' said Samantha, retreating back behind the counter. 'There's nothing wrong with giving people a touch of local colour.'

The man grunted a laugh, then did a slight double-take at Metka. 'Miss Benkovič,' he said. 'Hope your flat's working out?'

'Very well,' Metka replied. 'My landlady is very pleasant.'

'Excellent,' said the man, before nodding this time to Susan. 'Am I to take it you're working at Ashford Hall along with Miss Benkovič?'

'I am,' Susan replied guardedly.

The man fished inside another pocket before producing a business card and handing it to her. 'If you're ever looking for a place to rent, or even buy...'

Susan saw from the card that his name was Adam Phillips, a local estate agent. 'Thank you,' she said, 'but I have an AirBnB that serves me quite nicely.'

Phillips made a gagging sound, then smiled to show he meant

31

no offence. 'That's a shame,' he said, heading for the door. 'Keep the card in case you change your mind – house prices started to climb once Ashford announced he was investing in the area, and they're only going to climb higher after the Halls are officially open for business.' He pointed a finger at her and Metka. 'And don't listen to any nonsense about the spirit of some murdered girl wandering the corridors. Good day to you.'

'Arsehole,' Samantha muttered as he left, then cast a glance at Susan and Metka's empty plates. 'You done, then?'

Outside the café, the rain had turned misty. The two women walked a few feet up the road, then turned to each other and laughed.

'All that stuff that man said, about a girl being murdered,' asked Susan. 'Is that something that really happened at Ashford Hall?'

'It is,' Metka affirmed, zipping up her windbreaker and pushing her hands deep into its pockets. She nodded at her car. 'I can give you a lift to the Halls if you want.'

Susan hesitated just a moment too long, and Metka rewarded her with an appraising look. 'You're worried about something?'

About Andrew seeing me arriving with you? She cringed at the thought of him making another scene. If it wasn't for the fact that her project was almost on the rocks, she'd have asked Ashford to find her another project manager.

'Not a problem,' said Metka, pulling out her keys. 'You have your own car, of course-'

'No,' said Susan. 'Actually, it's in for repairs, so I've been getting a taxi into work. It'd be much easier if I just came with you.'

Susan began to regret her decision on discovering that the heating in Metka's car was broken. With all the wind and rain over the past few days, it felt more like February than July. Susan shivered in the passenger seat and pulled her coat tight around her.

'This girl who was murdered,' she asked, while Metka guided the Volkswagen out into the traffic, 'who was she?'

'Clara Ward,' Metka replied, the wheel sliding under her hands.

'And she's the one reputedly haunting the place?'

'Reputedly, yes.' Metka shrugged like it was the least of her concerns. 'Of course, unless her spirit comes up and introduces itself by name, we have no way of being certain.' She glanced sideways at Susan.

'Who was Clara Ward, exactly? Was she from Wardenby?'

Metka nodded. 'She was a young girl from the council estate.' The car took a right turn. 'She was just seventeen in 1987 when she was murdered by a down-and-out. Her body was found in the same room where you lost your shoe on Friday, as a matter of fact.'

Susan stared at her in shock. 'The *same* room?'

Metka nodded. 'Apparently kids from the estate would go to hang out in the ruins of the Halls to take drugs, drink, and screw.'

'I suppose now would be as good a time as any to ask how the place ended up in ruins.'

'It got hit by a German bomber dropping its payload during the Second World War. The Ashford's survived and built a new home on the other side of village.'

They passed out of the old part of Wardenby, which had started out as a village before a housing estate had been constructed on its south flank in the late 1960s. Soon they were in open countryside, low fells undulating around them. Ashford Hall came into view, looking much as it probably had in the years before the war.

'There's something I wanted to ask,' said Metka. 'You said you heard whistling coming from that room?'

'Yes.'

'Can you remember the melody?'

It seemed to Susan a strange thing to ask. 'I couldn't carry a tune if my life depended on it,' she replied, 'so the chances of me being able to sing it accurately are roughly zero. But a building like this probably has weird acoustics, especially given it's not really finished. It could have been the wind.'

Metka's expression suggested this was a far from adequate explanation. 'But it *sounded* like whistling?'

Susan didn't reply. Gravel spat from under the wheels of the car as they passed through gates beside which a sign had been erected proclaiming the arrival of Ashford Industries.

'Most of what we do,' said Metka, putting a particular stress on the word *most,* 'involves proving that something people claim is there actually isn't. Either way, we still have to set up cameras and microphones, EM meters and all the rest of it.'

They pulled up outside the building entrance. Rajam's car was already there, along with two vans, one belonging to the builders and the other to Professor Bernard.

Susan pushed the passenger-side door open, but stopped when Metka touched her elbow. 'If you have time,' she said, 'there are some recordings I would like you to listen to.'

Susan regarded her with suspicion. 'What kind of recordings?'

'EVP's.'

Susan shook her head in confusion, one foot on the gravel, the other still in the car. 'What?'

'Electronic Voice Phenomena,' Metka explained, getting out and looking at Susan over the roof of her car. 'They're purportedly recordings of the dead, speaking to each other. Ashford Hall is famous because of them.'

'Then... why haven't I heard of them before?'

'Well, you didn't know a girl was killed here, did you?'

'Well, no,' Susan admitted.

'Then you should look into the history of Ashford Hall,' Metka advised. 'It makes interesting reading. Most EVP's just prove people hear what they want to hear.' She nodded up at Ashford's newly reconstructed stonework and windows, most of which were dark. 'But the ones recorded here are a little more special than most.'

Another car pulled up beside them and Andrew got out. He cast a baleful eye towards Metka and nodded to her, his mouth set in a flat line of disapproval. He had a rolled-up newspaper gripped tightly in one hand. 'Miss Borovič,' he said.

'Doctor Wrigley.' Metka nodded back. 'I just gave your associate here a lift in.'

'Very good.' Andrew turned to Susan, his eyes full of roiling disapproval. 'Miss MacDonald? There's something we need to talk about.'

He marched inside the building without waiting for either of them. 'Not that bad?' asked Metka, regarded Susan with disbelief.

Susan's skin flushed with embarrassment. 'I take it back,' she said. 'He's a complete arsehole.'

They entered the main hall to find Andrew waiting there before the still-unmanned reception desk. Metka nodded briefly to them both before hurrying up the stairs and turning in to the West Wing.

'What did she want?' Andrew asked abruptly, as soon as Metka was out of earshot.

'None of your damn business,' she snapped. 'We ran into each other and had a coffee.'

He shook his head. 'I wouldn't advise being seen talking to either her *or* Bernard right now.'

'You're my project manager, not my boss,' she said, stabbing an outraged finger at his chest, 'something you seem to have forgotten. So if I want to –'

'You don't understand,' he said, holding up the newspaper. 'I don't *care* who the hell you have coffee with.' He slapped one end of the rolled-up newspaper into an open palm. 'It's because of what's in here.'

Susan stared at the newspaper with confusion. 'What about it?'

He nodded towards the staircase. 'Let's go up first. Rajam needs to hear about this as well.'

Andrew threw the newspaper down next to the kettle, then strode up to the window before turning to face them both. Rajam, who had been sitting at the workstation, pulled off his headphones and blinked at them both in a way that suggested he hadn't yet had his second coffee of the morning.

'Take a look,' said Andrew, nodding to the newspaper.

Susan picked it up. It was the Wardenby Advertiser, most of which usually consisted of small adverts and photos of local school fêtes and little in the way of real information. This time, however, a huge headline in red occupied most of the space above the fold: GHOST HUNTERS IN TOWN. Beneath the headline was the same photograph of Maxim Bernard that had been on Rajam's phone.

Susan carried it over to Rajam so he could take a look at it. 'A newspaper?' he asked, staring at it. 'I thought they'd gone the way of the horse and buggy. What's wrong with a website?'

Susan flipped to a half-page article on the third page and

scanned the columns. 'It's talking about whether or not Ashford is responsible for them being here.' She shook her head. 'My God,' she said in wonder, 'someone really did hold a séance. I thought maybe Ashford was kidding.'

'It's a bloody travesty!' Andrew shouted, startling both of them. 'It's making a *mockery* of us.'

'Andrew,' Susan said carefully, 'while I understand your concern, I do feel you're overreacting.'

'*Overreacting?*' He stared at her, his eyes bulging. 'What happens if this nonsense gets picked up by the Guardian – or, worse, the Daily Mail? Don't you see that if it gets out that Ashford's paid for a bunch of fucking woo-woo merchants to set up shop here, it throws everything else associated with him into disrepute?'

'It sounds to me,' Susan said levelly, 'as if you're much more concerned about getting your own project funded by Ashford.'

He glared at her. 'Look, I understand why you personally chose to accept Ashford's funding – because you got bilked out of co-authorship on your previous research. Well, believe me, however much you might hate academic rivalry, *this* stuff –' he stabbed a finger at the newspaper '– this dreamcatchers and spirit-energy bullshit, will stick to you for the rest of your career like burning mud. People will always question the veracity of your work purely by association.'

Susan started to formulate an angry reply, but couldn't, mainly because Andrew wasn't entirely wrong. 'An idiot made out of money, I think you said,' was the best she could do.

'I'm sorry for losing my temper,' he said, not sounding remotely sincere. 'You're right. I'm worried about my own project, and he's the only one who seemed remotely willing to fund it. But this...' He took the newspaper from her, crumpled it into a ball and threw it at a wall. 'This is too much.'

'Look,' she said, 'if it's out, it's out. I don't know what we can do about it. Ranting and raving isn't going to change that any, Andrew.'

He started suddenly and peered at her. 'Did that woman say anything to you about any of this?' he asked her. 'Was there any sign that she or Bernard or whoever might already have talked to the press?'

'None,' she assured him. 'If anything, I got the impression they're sober, scientific types, whatever their reasons for being here.'

'That I find hard to believe,' Andrew muttered. He appeared to have burned out most of his anger. He slumped onto the edge of a desk. 'But I do think it would be wise to keep an eye out for reporters.'

'I'm sure there won't be –'

'If it was interesting enough to get on that ridiculous rag's front page,' said Andrew, 'it'll be interesting to Fleet Street as well, mark my words.' He made a groaning sound. 'Dear God. I was telling an old friend just the other week how I was involved with some hush-hush corporate research, and now they're going to find out about it from the fucking astrology column in next week's Mirror.'

She glanced at Rajam, who had pushed his office chair back until it was wedged into the corner made by his desk and the wall. He looked deeply ill at ease.

'If we're even here next week,' Susan reminded him. 'It's been four or five days since we spoke with Ashford, and we're no further on now than we were then.'

'I guess you have a point,' said Andrew. 'But you've still got a few days before Ashford reviews your contract. What else do you want to try in the meantime?'

'Honestly?' Susan shrugged. 'Nothing.'

Andrew raised his eyebrows. 'Really?'

'Really,' she said. 'You know, I thought I was onto something, but... Maybe it's time for me to accept defeat. I'm not getting anywhere.'

'And you're absolutely sure about that?'

'I am,' said Susan. The finality of her own words hit Susan harder than she'd expected. 'We'd probably have had better luck with a pair of paper cups and a ten-thousand-mile long piece of string.'

Andrew laughed quietly. 'Well said, if unfortunate.' He stood up from the desk. 'In that case, I might take a few days to go down to London. It'd be an opportunity to find out about any alternative investors for my own research in case Ashford's exposed as a crank.

Unless you think you might need me around?'

'I think I'll be fine.' Susan waved a weary hand at him. 'If I need you for anything, I'll give you a call.'

Rajam stared mutely at the door after Andrew had left. 'Well,' he said at last, turning to Susan, 'do we start packing up, or...?'

She glanced towards the door behind which the Beast still lurked. 'Maybe not straight away,' she replied. 'Ashford said there might be something in all this that's patentable. I should probably check over my contract to see what it says about ancillary patents.' She frowned, then looked at Rajam. 'I got talking to one of the ghost-hunters,' she said, 'and she told me there'd been a murder right here in Ashford Hall. Did you know anything about that?'

'Clara Ward?' Rajam shrugged. 'Sure.'

She stared at him. 'Why on Earth didn't you mention it before?'

He regarded her with utter confusion. 'It's all there on Ashford Hall's Wikipedia page. Didn't you ever look?'

She blinked at him. 'Well... no.'

He gave her an exaggerated shrug, as if to say *don't blame me*.

'Fine,' she said with a sigh, and picked up the balled-up newspaper. She spread the page with the article out on her desk and glanced through it again. 'Did Wikipedia happen to mention anything about a séance?'

He turned and tapped at his computer, bringing up a browser. 'It did, actually. Apparently Clara Ward had a sister they asked to take part in it. The whole thing was organised by some occult society.' He peered at the screen. 'It says here there was some kind of controversy.'

'Really?'

'Yeah.' He clicked a hyperlink and the page changed. 'Says here they used a ouija board to try and contact the spirit of Clara Ward. There were a bunch of witnesses present, including some people from the area. Except every time they tried to get the ghost to write out its name, instead of writing *Clara*, it kept giving them Claire – that's the name of the dead girl's sister.'

'And you said she took part in the séance?'

'Uh-huh.' Rajam read some more of the Wikipedia entry. 'The whole thing was a total farce, and they even accused the sister of deliberately trying to screw the whole thing up.' Rajam leaned back and chuckled. 'Load of bullshit if you ask me.'

Tuesday July 7th 2020

The next day, a Tuesday, and just when she'd been debating whether it was worth even going in to Ashford Hall, Susan got a text message from Metka asking her to come and find her in the West Wing.

It was only then she remembered Metka's request that she should listen to recordings of ghosts. As ridiculous as it seemed, it at least gave her an opportunity to avoid thinking about the fate of her project. She showered, then walked from her rented flat to the garage where her car was waiting and drove it into work, with a quick stopover at the Karma Café to pick up a couple of coffees to go.

On her arrival, she discovered a new security guard at the front desk with a name tag that said Pat. She flashed him her Ashford Initiative ID before quickly introducing herself and making her way upstairs. There were now even more cables trailing up and down the South Wing passageway, and more microphones on stands scattered about the place.

She followed the cables to the West Wing, and a high-ceilinged room that smelled of fresh paint. Bernard, Metka and Angus had contrived to fill it with the paraphernalia of recording equipment. She saw several trestle tables arranged along a wall, supporting a variety of laptops, printers and monitors. There were cardboard boxes everywhere, spilling over with more cables and microphone booms.

Metka was there, with Professor Bernard, both of them studying some image on the screen of a MacBook. There was no sign of Angus. Susan rapped her knuckles on the frame of the open door to get their attention.

Bernard looked over, blinking with surprise. Susan held up the coffees and gave an apologetic shrug. 'Sorry I didn't get more than two.'

'Not to worry!' Bernard exclaimed, his voice reverberating from the unadorned walls. 'I don't drink the stuff anyway.'

Metka gestured to Susan to come in and gratefully accepted one of the coffees. 'I'm glad you came. I would like you to listen to something.'

Susan glanced at the laptop screen, and saw a grainy image of the same room where she'd found the bracelet. Metka tapped at the MacBook's keyboard, and the screen changed to show a waveform.

A hiss of static issued from a pair of enormous speakers sitting on either side of Metka like huge, black monoliths, loud enough to make Susan wince. In the midst of it Susan heard the sound of someone whistling, although it was almost lost amidst all the static.

'That's...' she began to say, then stopped.

Metka studied her carefully. 'Have you heard this particular melody before?'

'It does sound like what I heard the other day,' she admitted after a moment's thought.

Metka increased the volume slightly. 'Please be sure. Are you *certain?*'

'I think so,' said Susan. 'Is this an EVP? It's just someone whistling.'

'It is an EVP,' Metka confirmed. 'It was recorded twenty-six years ago, in 1994.'

Susan laughed uncertainly. 'Well, fair enough. But I don't see what that proves.'

Metka gave her a carefully measured look. 'I did mention to you that Ashford Hall is famous for such recordings. There are many more.'

Susan shrugged. 'It's just someone whistling. Look, I'm happy to help, but I'm not sure what you're aiming for.'

'The important thing,' Metka continued, 'is that it's what drew you to that room. And none of us have heard any such thing since we arrived here – not me, nor Bernard or Angus. It was not picked up by the microphones that were in the room at the time. Only *you* heard the whistling, Susan.'

'I mean...' Susan fumbled with her coffee, pulling the plastic lid off and sipping it, a sudden chill taking hold of her.

'Would you like,' Metka asked next, 'to hear a recording made while you were in that room, and just before I arrived there?'

'Metka,' said Bernard, a warning in his voice.

'I think she should hear it,' said Metka brusquely. 'You thought so yourself.'

'In principle, yes, but –'

'Is there a problem?' asked Susan.

'Not a problem, no.' Metka turned back to her. 'You say you don't believe in ghosts.' Susan nodded. 'Then may I ask, are you particularly religious in any way?'

Susan nearly laughed until she saw how serious she was. 'My family are technically Catholic, but they're the definition of "lapsed". I haven't been in a church since I was five years old.'

'So you don't have an objection to me playing this for you just now?'

Susan glanced uncertainly at Bernard, whose expression was carefully blank, and then back at Metka. 'I don't see why not.'

Metka nodded, then faced her computer. She selected another sound file and once again the room was filled with the hiss of static. Susan heard the sound of breathing, and footsteps.

'This is the moment you walked into the room,' explained Metka. She turned the volume up further. Susan heard the scuff of her shoes on plywood boards, loud enough it sounded like two icebergs scraping against each other.

Then she heard it again: a sound like an indrawn breath. She remembered the feeling of the tiny hairs on the nape of her neck reacting, as if someone's chill breath had touched her skin at that moment. That same chill now worked its way up her spine, wrapping icy tendrils around her lips and skull.

Then she heard another gasp – her own, when she had turned around thinking someone was there. She jumped at the sound of a sudden clattering noise, painfully loud.

'Sorry,' shouted Metka, pausing the audio. 'It has to be this loud. You'll understand why in a moment. What happened at that moment, do you remember?'

'Well, I thought I heard a sound like someone was about to say something, from right behind me,' she said. 'It startled me a little and I stumbled when I looked around and saw no one there.'

Metka nodded, and started the audio again, this time turning it even louder.

The recording of Susan's unsteady breathing filled the room, sounding like bellows as she dug around between the joists, first for her shoe, and then for the bracelet. The background hiss made her think of some tropical jungle caught in a deluge.

'Listen closely,' Metka shouted. 'Can you hear?'

Susan heard nothing but a din of static, except, perhaps, for a slight hiccup, as if it had been momentarily interrupted. 'I'm sorry,' she shouted, 'I can't. Really, this is just –'

'I'll change the settings,' Metka yelled, then rewound the audio. The recording screeched oddly as it ran backwards at speed. Bernard, who had gone to sit at another laptop and appeared to be writing someone an email, seemed entirely unfazed by the racket.

The hissing was deeper in tone this time, filling the room with a low rumble Susan could almost feel in her teeth. For a moment, she thought she could make something out – an *oo* followed by *aa*.

Metka rolled it back yet again, then forward, modulating the sound further. It sounded almost like a voice, saying *uff ath*.

Metka modulated it again.

Susan, a voice said.

She dropped her coffee. She thanked the Gods she'd put the plastic lid back on: even so, a little of it leaked across some of the cables. She snatched the cup back up and pressed the lid down tight before putting it down on a flat surface.

Metka had turned the sound off, and for the first time Susan understood what a deafening silence was. 'No need to worry,' said

Bernard, snatching a cloth up from his desk and mopping up the spilt coffee.

'What the hell *was* that?' asked Susan. 'Where did that voice-'

'Keep listening,' said Metka, and played the recording again.

Susan stared hard at Metka, afraid some kind of elaborate trick was being played on her. *Susan*, the recording said again, somehow much clearer now Metka had modified it. The name repeated with the regularity of a heartbeat. *Susan. Susan. Susan.*

Susan found herself moving backwards until her back was pressed up against the door, her hand over her mouth.

Then the voice changed, saying: *Susan, he'll kill me. He'll kill me, Susan. He'll kill me...*

She fled, running out into the corridor. The next thing she knew, she was back at the top of the grand staircase, looking down at the security desk and breathing hard.

Suddenly the very last thing she wanted was to be anywhere near Ashford Hall. She heard Metka calling after her, and it spurred her into action, sending her clattering down the stairs and past the security guard, who looked at her curiously as she fled outside.

Then she got in her car and put as much distance between herself and that voice as she could.

That same Tuesday evening, Susan received two emails: one from Rajam, and one from Metka. Rajam's said since she hadn't come in that day, he'd gone ahead with writing up some research notes and doing some routine maintenance. Metka's email, by contrast, took the form of an apology.

Soon after, Metka called her on her mobile phone.

'I hope you don't mind, but I got your number from Rajam this morning. I know that this may not be to the fore of your thoughts at this moment, but I do think there are some things we should talk about.'

'That recording you played me,' said Susan. 'It was faked, wasn't it?'

'It was not faked,' Metka insisted somewhat testily. 'As much as you might prefer it were not the case, I swear what I played to you is real. Just give me half an hour to explain. If you don't agree something extraordinary is happening here, I will never bring it up again. Do you know the Grey Lady?'

One of Wardenby's two pubs, in the village's original high street. 'I know it, yes. But I'm far from sure –'

'Meet me there at eight.'

She found Metka in an alcove towards the back of the Grey Lady's lounge, far from the loud chatter of the main bar. Metka sat with a half-finished shepherd's pie in front of her, a pair of Bose earphones clamped over her ears and a laptop screen illuminating her features. A poster above her announced an upcoming performance by a band called The Stone Tapes.

When Metka looked up, her expression made it clear she hadn't been sure whether Susan would actually turn up. In truth, neither had Susan.

'You're going to have to try very hard,' said Susan, sitting across from Metka without taking off her coat, 'to convince me what I heard this afternoon wasn't some crappy audio from a horror movie.'

'I can't prove that,' said Metka. 'All I can do is give you my word. Our sound equipment is highly sensitive and it was recording the whole time you were in there. You told me that the whistling you heard, but which wasn't picked up by our microphones, sounded the same as a recording made in that same room many years ago. For the moment at least, are you willing to accept that?'

'Perhaps,' said Susan. 'For the moment, anyway.' She relaxed enough to sit back from where she was perched on the edge of her seat. 'But I have to remain sceptical – *very* sceptical. You must understand why.'

'Of course.' Metka nodded. 'One has to be, regarding such matters.'

'All right,' asked Susan, 'all these recordings you've been telling me about – they date back to Clara Ward's murder?'

'Yes. The first was made just days after she died. A hundred more were recorded over the next twenty-five years, with the one I played you being the most recent. If you want to know more about them, there are numerous online articles as well as academic research.'

Susan picked up a menu with a sigh and began to unbutton her coat. 'You have no idea just how much you unnerved me.'

'Sorry.' She sounded like she meant it. 'There is more I would like to play to you, if you would allow me.' She put up a hand. 'Only whenever you are ready.'

'I really feel like I've had enough of that kind of thing for a lifetime. And...' she sighed. 'I don't think I'll be at Ashford Hall much longer, so I probably won't be able to help you as much as you clearly think I can.'

Metka's brow crinkled into a frown. 'Your research is complete?'

'Not exactly. I...' She dropped the menu back down. 'Our experiment didn't work. In fact, the whole thing's turned out to be an utter waste of time.'

'Oh.' Metka regarded her with some sympathy. 'I'm sorry to hear that.'

Not as sorry as I am, thought Susan.

'I think,' said Metka, 'I owe you a dinner, if you haven't eaten. First I scare you half out of your pants, then I drag you all the way here. Besides, it's cheap. Allow me, please.'

Susan saw no reason to object. 'I make a terrible dinner companion,' she said. 'I have a reputation for talking about nothing but work. I'm very boring, I'm afraid.'

'Nonsense.' Metka waved to a passing member of the bar staff and Susan ordered a pie and chips. 'If you don't mind,' asked Metka, 'how did you come to work for Ashford?'

'Well, after I graduated, I went to the States to do my PhD and managed to get myself into the junior faculty at UCLA for two years. I ended up working on experiments involving quantum entanglement.'

Metka nodded. 'Spooky action at a distance.'

'Well, we had some odd results involving an experiment I was assisting on. That led me to wonder if there might be something in there that demonstrated retrocausality.'

Metka nodded, and began picking at the remains of her own meal. 'Information going backwards in time, you said.'

'To when a pair of particles were first entangled, yes. And then it goes forward again. I shared my findings with two senior researchers on the project because I needed more time to test and verify my results.'

'And?'

Susan sighed, unpleasant memories quickly resurfacing. 'To cut a long story short, they carried out their own tests and published before me and without my knowledge.'

'Isn't that like... stealing your work?'

'Not exactly, no. I had every right to publish my own paper if I wanted, except their having seniority over me pretty much guaranteed their paper would get published well in advance of anything I could come up with, and get a lot more attention. And by the time I did finally publish something, it would be old news.'

Metka frowned. 'I would have kicked up a fuss.'

'Yes,' said Susan, picking up a knife and fork as her pie and chips arrived. 'Unfortunately, that's exactly what I did.'

'"Unfortunately"?'

Susan's fist tightened around the knife in her hand as she sawed a chip in half. 'I got told everything I just told you – that they had every right to do what they did, just like I had every right to write my own paper. So I thought, fine. I'll forget about it. Besides, my work was solid, or so I believed. Except when it came time to review my contract, they kicked me out.'

Metka regarded her thoughtfully. 'And you think it's because you complained?'

'I think it's because I didn't regularly play golf with members of the review board, like certain senior researchers did.' She shook her head. 'I really thought I was onto something, Metka. I really did.'

'So what will you do next,' Metka asked, 'if your experiment is over?'

'I'll go in to take some final readings and write a final report, but after that we'll have to start dismantling everything.'

Metka took a deep breath, as if she needed to get her courage up before speaking. 'I was perhaps not entirely truthful with you when I asked you to meet me here.'

Susan looked up at her, her mouth full of chips and pie. 'Oh?'

The other woman smiled apologetically. 'While I was getting your email and phone number from Rajam, he showed me the machine you built.'

'The Beast?'

Metka chuckled quietly. 'Beauty and the Beast – it's really very clever, the names. Anyway, it reminded me of something, and... well, I would be very remiss if I didn't at least ask you to listen to something again.'

Susan stared at the laptop and headphones next to Metka's elbow with alarm and put her knife and fork down. 'Oh God, Metka. You're not going to ask me to listen to *another* of those ghastly recordings?'

'Please,' said Metka, pushing her dish aside and pulling her laptop close. 'I understand your reticence, but what I have here is quite, quite different from what I played you this morning. It's a recording dating from 1992.' She plugged her headphones into the laptop, then passed the headset over to Susan. 'I promise you, if you think nothing of it, I will never bother you with these matters again or ever even mention them. I swear. But I truly believe you'll regret not hearing this.'

Susan's gut told her to thank the woman and leave, but instead she let Metka push the headphones into her hands.

'Just to be clear,' Susan reminded her, 'I don't believe in any of this shit. I only even came along this morning because I couldn't face going into work.'

'Then believe in the evidence of your ears,' said Metka. She touched a noise-reducing switch on the side of the headphones as Susan, with some reluctance, put them on, still unable to shake the sense that she was falling for some horrendously complicated confidence trick.

With the headphones on, the background rumble of conversation from the main bar faded to almost nothing. She watched, hesitant and fearful, as Metka's fingers moved across the keyboard of her computer.

She heard a hiss, growing louder. Then came a deep bass rumbling that might have been a voice, but muffled and far from audible.

She reached up to take the headphones off and tell Metka she could make nothing out, when the voice became suddenly much clearer.

It's not too late for Beauty, a man's voice said. She could just about make the words out over the hiss. *I think they're ready to take over.* Then, after a pause, *We don't have to tell Susan yet.*

She tore the headphones off and stood up. 'It's been nice talking to you,' she said, her voice taut and harsh, 'but this is the last straw. I've had enough of –'

While she spoke, Metka turned her laptop around so Susan could see the screen. It showed a black and white photograph of a tumbled ruin, and a headline reading SPOOKY RUMBLINGS AT ASHFORD HALL.

'Read this,' said Metka, pointing at one particular paragraph. 'This is an archive page from the Daily Mirror, dated 28 February 1992. Do you see what it says?'

Susan sat down slowly and read it.

Amongst the spooky goings-on, according to Arthur Melville, chairman of the Brighton Tulpa Society, are audio recordings of ghostly visitations. "Most of them appear meaningless on the surface," Arthur told our reporter, "but we think perhaps restless spirits are trying to communicate something important to us. That's why we in the Society feel it's vital to keep track of these voices, and the things they tell us."

Arthur is also the organiser behind a séance due to be held in the ruins of Ashford Hall, which burnt down nearly fifty years ago after being hit by a stray German bomb. The spooks apparently like to say things like "The Beast is failing, it's not too late for Beauty, and we don't have to tell Susan yet." Susan, unfortunately, was not available for comment.

'You could still have made that up,' Susan said weakly.

Metka stared at her. 'Of course. I dug into the Daily Mirror's archives and inserted fake historical documentation. I also snuck into the British Archives and inserted fake information about the same recording into dozens of recorded reports and widely distributed articles on Ashford Hall EVPs.' She arched one eyebrow. 'And used your time machine to go back and do it.'

'It could still be some weird coincidence.' Susan realised her heart was thundering in her chest. 'And it doesn't exactly sound like a natural conversation, does it?'

'No, it doesn't,' Metka agreed. 'Although few EVP's do. But even so, what I just played you is not the full recording. The original is much longer, with very long pauses between each statement. I can play the original recording for you if you like, but we'd be here for a while.'

'No.' Susan shook her head. It wasn't an experience she had the remotest desire to repeat. 'Besides, it's just one recording. That makes it nothing more than a coincidence.'

'But it *isn't* the only recording,' Metka reminded her. 'I told you there are dozens more, and several of those contain the same words and phrases, recorded between the time of Clare Ward's murder and shortly before the renovation and reconstruction work began on Ashford Hall.'

'Recorded how, exactly?' Susan asked. 'And by whom?'

'Recorded by people who have an interest in such things. The man in the article, Arthur Melville, is the head of a group called the Tulpa Society. They have an extensive collection of their own recordings. Melville allowed us access to them when we told him we were coming to Ashford Hall.'

'Look,' said Susan, regaining some of her composure, 'even if you somehow managed to convince me any of this meant something, the fact is being involved with parapsychologists might cost me my career.' *What's left of it, anyway.*

'But don't you see?' Metka insisted. 'There is a clear connection between these recordings and your work!'

Susan shook her head in confusion. 'How could you possibly figure that?'

Metka sighed as if Susan were an obstinate schoolchild unable to grasp a simple concept. 'You *said* you were sending information back in time, is that correct?'

'Yes,' Susan agreed. 'That's what we were *trying* to do. But even if we'd succeeded, the information would only have travelled backwards in time by a few seconds. That's barely enough time to blink.'

'I apologise if what I say next seems ridiculous to you,' said Metka. 'You undoubtedly have a much deeper understanding of these matters than I do. But I could not help but wonder – might it be possible that your experiment *is* working, but instead of going back in time by microseconds, the information contained within your particles is somehow instead travelling back many years into the past?'

'That's ridic –' Susan paused mid-word, thinking.

'I admit it seems like a silly idea,' said Metka, 'and I realise I'm hardly qualified to –'

'No,' said Susan, putting up a hand to shush her. 'Hold on.'

Was such a thing really possible, as outrageous as it sounded, she wondered? Except the messages they were trying to send between Beauty and the Beast were hardly messages in the sense Metka or most people meant: they were more like packets of data containing coordinate information related to the time and place of each experiment. There were certainly no cryptic voice messages involved.

Susan poked at the remains of her food, but her hunger was gone. 'Did you ever hear of a man called Percival Lowell?'

Metka shook her head. 'Back in the 1870s,' Susan explained, 'Lowell looked through a telescope and saw dark lines on the surface of Mars. He managed to convince himself these were evidence of canals built by some ancient Martian civilisation. Except, of course, they weren't anything of the kind.'

'I don't see how –'

'The point is, *he saw what he wanted to see*. And you're trying to tell me that somehow I'm sending messages possibly decades back into the past, where they get picked up by some kook sitting around in a bunch of rubble in the rain with a tape recorder?'

Metka regarded her levelly. 'Then how do *you* explain it?'

'I don't know. But here's the thing: that recording you played me back at Ashford Hall, from when I was in that room and I lost my shoe, wasn't some message from the future. That sounded like someone – or some*thing* – speaking to me directly. Which either means Ashford Hall is haunted by an actual ghost, or someone is trying to convince me it is. That makes it two separate phenomena, do you see? On the one hand, we have messages from the future – our present – meaning it's a physical phenomenon, unrelated to the supernatural. But on the *other* hand,' Susan continued, waving her fork at Metka, 'we have that... *voice*, whispering to me like...' She shuddered and put the fork down again.

'All right,' asked Metka. 'Then what do you think is going on?'

That you're lying to me, thought Susan. *I'm thinking that you and Bernard and Angus are working for Christian Ashford in some capacity that has nothing to do with parapsychology.* It was the simplest explanation, and therefore the most likely one.

But then again, even if that were the case, *why?*

It just didn't make sense.

She glanced at her watch and saw it was very nearly ten pm. The realisation sent a wave of fatigue through her. 'I'll sleep on it,' Susan said, getting up. 'Maybe I'll think of something. And thank you for the meal.'

Instead of going home, Susan drove back to Ashford Hall.

She saw only a few lights were on inside the mansion as she drove up the long driveway. Even so, it was clear the building was far from unoccupied. The builder's van was parked outside, and she heard the distant whine of a drill as she got out and locked her car.

There was another new security guard at the reception when she walked in. 'You're working late,' he said when she showed him her pass.

'So are you.' He sat with his shoulders hunched, and there were dark circles under his eyes. 'Hope you're getting enough sleep,' she added.

He chuckled nervously. 'Always been a light sleeper. Night watchman's best job for the likes of me.'

'I won't be long,' she assured him, and nodded towards the upper floor. 'I'm in the East Wing.'

'Right you are.' He nodded, and darted a sideways look at the stairs as if he was afraid to look too long. 'I won't be bothering you.'

She made her way upstairs and into the room containing the Beast, pulling a seat up next to the long table on which the array was mounted so she could stare at it beneath the strip lights. Most likely, Ashford or one of his associates would give them at least a couple of days to dismantle all the equipment, but it still meant she was going to be looking for a new job by the end of next week. She could even get started on dismantling it now, if she wanted...

But that wasn't what was on her mind. All she could think about was everything Metka had said. And try as she might, she could find no possible motive for Metka to play an elaborate trick on her. And that, in turn, led Susan to at least consider the idea that – *somehow* – the array really was sending snatches of apparently random conversation backwards through time.

But that, in turn, raised even bigger questions. How, for instance, could the Array pick up audible sound, something it wasn't designed to do? Why should that sound be audible inside Ashford Hall, at different points in the past, instead of in some other, entirely separate location? Did that mean there was something inside the building that acted as a focus for the information?

Like someone reading our mail, Andrew had said. Something able to observe and thereby decohere the quantum data by some unknown means...

She shook her head. The more she thought about it, the more unlikely the whole thing seemed.

She got up again and went back through to her desk, rummaging around inside it for a data stick that contained a backup of their test transmissions. Instead, her hand found the bracelet. She took it out, turning it this way and that, and noticed for the first time the letters *CW & CA FVR* had been scratched into the inner surface of the plate with a jeweller's drill.

How did I ever miss that? But then again, she'd almost entirely forgotten about the bracelet. She wondered who...

A thrill of revelation ran through her: *CW* might be Clara Ward, and *CA* –

She laughed at the idea. "CA" couldn't possibly stand for Christian Ashford. All of Metka's talk about séances and ghostly voices had sent her imagination out of control. And even if by some remote chance there really were some connection between Ashford and Clara Ward, there was no reason to think it was of any significance whatsoever. They had both grown up in Wardenby within the same time period, so it was logical and reasonable to assume they had known or at least been aware of each other.

She sat down in front of Rajam's workstation and googled the details of Clara Ward's death. A few minutes browsing informed her that the girl had been found dead of strangulation in the then-ruins of Ashford Hall, in August 1987. Worse, an autopsy had shown she was three months pregnant when she died. A local down-and-out named Brian Tull with a record of sexual assaults had been arrested and jailed before committing suicide in his cell a few years later. Ward had left behind a sister and elderly mother, both living in the nearby estate.

Should she, she wondered, take the bracelet to the police? But what possible use could they make of it? The murderer had been caught, after all, and Clara Ward had been dead for thirty-three years now.

Susan, he'll kill me.

She shuddered and put the bracelet down again, as if it had burned her skin. Even assuming the voice was real, why on Earth would it say such a thing?

She had heard a sound and followed it to that exact room, in a building that contained dozens of identical rooms. Why *that* one?

Had the same voice that whispered to her tried to lead her there?

'You're on a slippery slope if you start believing this stuff, my girl,' she said out loud to the empty room.

She picked the bracelet up and carried it over to a waste bin, standing over it and wondering why she couldn't bring herself to throw it away.

'Fine,' she said to it with a shuddering breath. 'You win.'

She pocketed the bracelet, got her coat and keys, and left.

Wednesday July 8th 2020

The next morning, on the way into Ashford Hall, Susan stopped at the Karma Café. She found Samantha busy in conversation with a pair of elderly women and waited until they were gone before ordering a latte to go.

'About what you were saying the other day,' Susan asked, over the noise of the coffee-grinder.

'Yeah?' Samantha glanced at her.

'I just wondered if you knew anything more about the, um, the haunting, up at Ashford Hall.'

Samantha gave her a knowing look. 'Like what, exactly?'

Susan repeated most of what Rajam had told her, and Samantha nodded. 'Honest, love, that's about the sum total of what I've heard, apart from a bit of an odd feeling whenever I'm anywhere near the place. Which is as little as I can manage,' she added. 'You should read the book about it.'

'What book? You mean Christian Ashford's autobiography?'

She blinked at Susan in incomprehension, then laughed, shaking her head. 'Sorry, took me a moment. God, no, that's a pile of utter crap. No, the book I'm thinking of is called, let's see...' She finished making the coffee and sealed it with a plastic lid before passing it over to Susan in return for a handful of change. '"The Haunting of Ashford Hall", I think. Written by some bloke called David...

something-or-other. Read it yonks ago.'

'Thanks.' Susan headed for the door.

'Might be out of print,' Samantha called after her. 'Heard the bloke who wrote it got in a bit of bother over it.'

Susan sat behind the wheel of her car, sipping the coffee and browsing Amazon on her phone. The author was David Summerfield, and the book was not only out of print, the lowest price she could find was over seventy-five pounds. Neither were there any electronic versions.

'Fuck that,' Susan muttered under her breath, then googled to try and find the nearest library. It had to be worth a shot.

It transpired that Susan had driven past Wardenby's sole library almost every day to and from work without realising it. It was housed inside a boxy grey concrete building near the motorway that separated Wardenby proper from the council estate. One side of the building had been defaced with graffiti. The only suggestion it might be a library was in a small, rather nondescript sign on the wall that Susan would never have noticed as she drove past.

The only occupants, apart from a small and mousy-looking female librarian, were a couple of elderly retirees browsing the romance section and several men who weren't much younger taking advantage of some ageing PCs. Susan hunted around until she found the history shelves, which were predominantly stocked with locally published books about the surrounding area. She did find a single copy of Ashford's autobiography, however. He gazed out from the cover photo with a wide grin that looked more than anything like an advert for some high-end cosmetic dental practice.

She figured she might as well find something out about the man before he cut her loose and carried it over to the library counter. The woman librarian had her back turned, and was busy feeding paper into a photocopier.

'Excuse me,' asked Susan, 'I'm trying to find a particular book. It's by an author called David...'

The woman turned and blinked owlishly at her. 'David who?'

Damn. 'I've forgotten it already,' she said sheepishly. 'Hang on.'

She put her rucksack on the counter and rooted around inside it to try and find her phone. She pulled out a scarf, a notebook, and finally the bracelet, placing them in an untidy pile on the counter before she managed to retrieve her phone and look at the last page she'd visited.

'Sorry,' she said, holding up her phone. 'I had it and it went right out my head. The author's name is David Summerfield.'

The librarian, however, wasn't listening. Instead, she had picked up the bracelet, turning it this way and that.

'Miss?'

The librarian seemed to suddenly remember where she was and put the bracelet back down, her skin several shades paler than it had been just a moment before. 'I'm sorry,' she said. 'Yes, I think I know what you're looking for. I'll just get it for you.'

'Oh! Well, if you just tell me where I can-' but the woman had already darted out from behind the counter and hurried off into the stacks.

Susan put the bracelet in her pocket and waited until the woman returned with a copy of *The Haunting of Ashford Hall* in one hand. The cover appeared even more lurid than it had online.

'Your library card?' the woman asked, taking the Ashford autobiography from her. There was a slight tremor to her voice, and she wouldn't meet Susan's gaze.

Susan suddenly realised she didn't have one. Or rather, her last library card, good only for libraries in Glasgow, was buried in a box somewhere in her parent's home in Cardonald.

She grinned with embarrassment. 'I don't seem to have –'

'Or some form of ID?'

Susan rooted around in her bag again and produced her driver's licence. The librarian studied it for what felt like a long time. 'Susan MacDonald,' she said at last, passing it back over. 'Where did you find that bracelet?'

'In Ashford Hall,' said Susan, befuddled. 'I found it under some floorboards. But I don't think we've ever me –'

'I see.' The librarian hurriedly passed over a slip of paper with a local authority web address on it. 'You can sign up online.' She pushed the Ashford book and the Summerfield back towards Susan.

Susan blinked at her. 'But don't you need to stamp them?'

'I can't, if you're not a member of the library yet.' The librarian's expression was hard and angry.

'Thank you,' Susan managed to mumble. 'I'll go online and get a membership.'

'There's no need,' said the woman, one hand clutching at her throat. 'Keep them if you want. Just... go.' She turned, then, and walked into a glass-walled office behind the desk, the door banging shut.

Susan stood there, utterly perplexed, and became gradually aware that several of the library's denizens were looking at her. She hurriedly tucked the books inside her rucksack and fled.

When she arrived at Ashford Hall, she found Pat manning the reception desk. 'I met your friend on the night shift last night,' she said.

'Dan? He quit.'

She looked at him in surprise. 'But didn't he just start?'

'He did, a week ago. Or was it two?' He shrugged. 'Anyway, he handed in his notice this morning. Agency says there'll be someone new by tonight.'

Susan nodded, unsettled. She started to move towards the stairs then paused and looked back at him. 'If you don't mind me asking, how are you finding the job?'

'Well...' His eyes darted away from her and he flashed her a tight smile. 'Hardly started myself, really. Seems good enough.'

'No bumps in the night?' she asked. 'I heard some stories about the place.'

He grinned, but she still caught the flash of fear in his eyes. 'Well, the agency did a great job of keeping quiet on all that when they offered me the job, but no. I'm day-shift only.'

'So did Dan say why he quit?'

His grin faded entirely and he shivered. 'He told me –' He stopped abruptly and darted her a wary look. 'Never mind. It's all loony nonsense.'

'What did he mention?' she persisted. 'Voices, maybe, or someone whistling?'

His eyes widened. 'So you –' he caught himself before he could say anything more.

'Have *you* heard something?' she asked on a sudden hunch.

'Just at the end of my shifts,' he admitted, his neck flushing red. 'I told that ghost-botherer all about it.'

'Bernard? You spoke to him?' She supposed he would have.

He nodded upwards. 'They played me all these noises and hisses and things. Creeped the hell out of me almost as much as the real thing.' He sighed and shook his head. 'Might as well tell you. I've decided to quit as well.'

'Really? It's that bad?'

'No, just... Sometimes I hear a crash or something, or what might be someone talking, and I have to go check it out and there's never anyone there. Or sometimes I'm sitting here and I could *swear* there's someone right behind me, or I can feel someone's breath on my shoulder. It's just...' He shuddered, then gave her an apologetic grin. 'I'd like to say I'm made of sterner stuff, but if I'm going to be scared I'd rather it's because I watched a box set of Exorcist movies.'

She nodded. 'Thanks for telling me.'

She made her way up the grand staircase and stood for a moment at the corridor leading to the South Wing. It was utterly silent. The sun came through paned windows at the far end, painting the varnished floorboards with light. Maxim Bernard's microphones still stood here and there along the corridor, as if waiting for a performance – which, in a sense, they were.

Susan spent the rest of that morning writing up some notes. For once, it was a warm day, and she went outside to sit in the sun and eat her lunch and read some of David Summerfield's book. Andrew was still down in London, and Rajam had caught the train to Taskerlands to spend the evening with his brother and his new niece.

From the book, she discovered that Ashford Hall had originally been haunted by an apparition known as the Grey Lady, although the most recent sighting was from the 1830s, and that from a maid reportedly given to "ecstasies of a religious nature". Summerfield was more concerned, however, with events immediately following the murder of Clara Ward.

The first reports of aural manifestations appeared only days after her death, and came mostly from the same kids given to hanging out amidst the ruins. That might have been the end of it until one of them recorded a manifestation on his Walkman, which in turn drew the attention of Arthur Melville and his Brighton-based Tulpa Society.

Over the next couple of years, the ruins became a goldmine for EVP recordings, some of which, according to Summerfield, were still renowned in certain esoteric circles for their clarity. Summerfield spent a whole chapter on the séance, which had been organised by Melville. And, as Rajam had noted, the dead girl's sister had been involved as well. Susan didn't have a sister, but if she had, she couldn't imagine doing any such thing.

There were pictures in the centrefold of the book showing the then-ruined grand staircase, the main hall open to the elements. There were also, naturally, pictures of the room where the murder had taken place. Photographs of the outside of the building showed the West Wing completely gone, while the East Wing stood barren and silent with long rows of empty, shadowy windows.

There were pictures of Clara as well, a school portrait that showed her with her tie askew, and teased blonde hair above a slightly vacant smile. Another showed her wearing a leather jacket and jeans and leaning against a motorbike, trying to look tough and utterly failing.

There were no pictures of Claire Ward, but she had been only fifteen when her sister died. Susan wondered what it must have been like to be a scared young woman surrounded by people claiming they could talk to her sister in the afterlife. The séance had employed a ouija board, with Melville asking questions and some presumably unseen spirit moving the pointer beneath their collective fingers.

When asked for its identity, the ghost had insisted its name was Claire Ward, not Clara Ward – even though Claire Ward herself had been sitting right there. That, in turn, led to accusations from some, although not Melville, the organiser, that she had deliberately "thrown" the séance. Which, given she was still young and presumably still processing the violent murder of her older sister, struck Susan as unconscionably cruel.

Up until this point, there had been surprisingly little mention of Christian Ashford beyond an acknowledgement of him as the last living member of his family. She flipped back through the book to find the date of publication was several years before Ashford struck lucky with a series of tech investments in California. But, as was clear, he had been living near Wardenby at the time of Clara's death, in the house his parents had bought before they died.

One paragraph in particular made her sit up: *I've already alluded to Christian Ashford's involvement with the local drug scene,* Summerfield wrote, *the details of which are a matter of public record. He was arrested twice, first in September 1986 and then in March 1987, in both cases on charges of possession of marijuana and amphetamines with intent to supply. Christian was a familiar sight in Wardenby at the time, often to be found sitting in the Grey Lady or roaring around the local countryside on his bright red two-stroke Suzuki.*

That Christian Ashford was in all other respects the archetypal rich kid goes without saying: he hardly needed the money he made from dealing, but thrived on playing fast and loose with the law. On the surface, at best, he appears to be no more than a peripheral player in the story of Clara Ward, to whom he almost certainly sold marijuana and amphetamines on a regular basis; traces of both of which were found in her blood following her autopsy.

There are, however, some aspects that have not been fully explained to date. Christian's alibi for the night in question remains that he was drinking in Soho with some of his Oxbridge chums. Yet there are those in Wardenby who claim to have seen someone wearing Christian's trademark leathers roaring down a road leading away from Ashford Hall on his familiar cherry-red Suzuki in the small hours of the morning following Clara's death. And can there be any truth to the persistent rumours that he had been the lover of both Claire and Clara Ward, without the knowledge of either party?

Christ, thought Susan, putting the book down. Summerfield had all but accused Ashford of being at the scene of Clara's murder.

By now, the day was heading towards late afternoon. She picked up the book and carried it back inside and took one last look at the Beast before packing everything into her rucksack and heading for the door.

Back in her rented flat, she ate a microwave dinner before picking up Ashford's autobiography. Even a glance at the first pages made it clear the book was more hagiography than objective journalism. She flipped through to some colour inserts that included a blurry Polaroid of a much younger Christian Ashford posing in front of his Suzuki. He had shoulder-length hair and bike leathers, and looked just the kind of man to lead a teenage girl astray.

Even so, Ashford's life in England, prior to his departure for California, was covered in a bare half-dozen pages, and his drug convictions got no more than a couple of sentences. The way it read, one might easily have come away with the notion that Ashford's drug-dealing career had taken place over a couple of weeks, and had been little more than a tentative brush with the law. Yet Summerfield's book showed he'd been dealing drugs in the area for at least two years by the time of his first arrest.

After that, it seemed as if Ashford's life consisted of one grand success after another. The front cover had a red sticker proclaiming it the number one bestselling business autobiography of 2015.

She fell asleep on her couch with the book open beside her, then jerked awake several hours later to find she had a text message from Rajam, asking her to meet him at the Grey Lady as soon as possible. Which was strange, because he was supposed to be in Taskerlands.

Susan found Rajam sitting in another alcove near the one she'd occupied with Metka the previous night. He was sitting with his elbows on the table, staring sideways at a TV mounted above the bar, shovelling crispy noodles into his mouth.

'I hope you're not about to tell me you've been harbouring secret feelings for me all this time,' she said, sliding into a seat across from him.

He made a snorting sound as if this was the most hilarious thing she could possibly have said, then put his fork down. 'I cancelled,' he said, swallowing a mouthful of noodles. 'I decided to visit my brother next week. I just didn't think it was right to leave you in the dark.'

'What are you talking about?' she asked, feeling a stab of

apprehension.

'Just to be clear,' he said, 'I don't want to get in any trouble over this.'

Dread descended over her like a dank fog. 'For God's sake, spit it out, Raj. What is it?'

He sighed, drawing it out. 'Christian Ashford called me and offered me a job.'

'Oh.' Why on Earth would he think that was bad news? 'Well, that's great, Rajam. I'm pleased for you. I mean, we're almost certainly done here, so –'

'No.' He shook his head. 'You don't understand. He told me some things but said I had to keep them in strictest confidence, or I could –' at this, he actually glanced from side to side, as if afraid someone might be listening '– I could get in legal trouble. So I'm not even supposed to be here talking to you. But I had to, do you see?'

'I'm not sure I do,' she said, her apprehension swiftly returning at a gallop.

'He wants to keep your project going,' said Rajam. 'He doesn't want to end it.'

She blinked at him. 'So... that's a *good* thing, isn't it? Why would you get in trouble because...?'

'He wants to keep it going *without* you. He offered me a job to keep working on the Beast after you're gone.'

'Without...' She leaned towards him, the roar of blood in her head louder even than the football match on the TV. 'How is that even possible?' she demanded, outraged.

'Ashford said something about having sunk too much money into the project to want to scrap it altogether. He wants to work on the potential patents associated with it, however, and he needs me, he says, because I know the array inside-out. He told me not to say one word to you.'

'Oh my God,' she muttered in dismay.

He nodded sympathetically. 'He's intending to give you your notice this coming Friday.' He shook his head violently. 'I just don't think it's right. I'd get a lawyer to take a look at your contract's fine print and find out *exactly* what it says you can or can't do about this.

It's *your* project, and it feels to me like he's trying to stop you knowing what's going on, or maybe preventing you getting any credit from any patents that might come out of the project.'

'I promise I won't tell anyone what you just told me,' she said with deep-felt gratitude. *Of all the underhand...*

She thought, then, of her conversation with Metka, of the things Pat the security guard had said and the voices in the recordings. As dismissive as she had been, she knew she was coming around to the idea that *something* was going on she didn't quite understand. Metka had started it by suggesting there might be a connection between the aural manifestations and her own work.

What if Metka had hit on something, she wondered? What if there were some hidden variable underlying entanglement nobody had ever found evidence for before – and her experiment was the first tangible proof of its existence?

It was an outrageous idea, but with so few days left, perhaps, before Ashford found a way to eject her from her own experiment, just what did she have left to lose?

'What do I have to lose?'

'Sorry?' Rajam was staring at her. 'Lose what?'

'Nothing,' Susan said breathlessly, feeling in that moment as if she were standing on the edge of a precipice. 'I need to go. Thank you.' She stood and came around the table and kissed Rajam's stubbled cheek. He blushed like a five-year old being fawned over by an elderly aunt.

'Hey,' he said, his voice suddenly gruff. 'No fraternising with the staff.'

'Absolutely,' she said, pulling her coat back on. 'I'll leave you and your noodles in peace.'

Back home, she dug out her contract and skimmed through it rapidly. The phrasing seemed worded just vaguely enough that perhaps Ashford *could* keep a project going without the permission or involvement of the person who'd instigated it. *The devil is always in the details*, she thought: she'd need a lawyer, and a good one, to even begin to make sense of all the legalese.

She leaned back from her kitchen table where she'd been sitting with the radio playing quietly in the background. If she took Ashford to court, she'd not only be facing off against a billionaire, she'd just be proving to the scientific community at large that she was still more interested in picking fights than carrying out research. Either way, she'd lose.

She opened her laptop and checked her email: no word yet from Ashford about the fate of her project. It was late Wednesday night, and there was still a chance Ashford wouldn't make any firm decisions until the start of next week.

So that gave her possibly the entire weekend to look into Metka's ideas.

Susan next tried calling Metka, but got a recorded message saying she'd be out of town until Friday. She left a message, then stared around her kitchen and realised there was no way she could just sit there for the rest of the night. She had to *do* something.

But what?

She picked up the David Summerfield book and flipped it over, finding a photograph of a rumpled-looking man in his early forties, wearing a thick cardigan over a creased shirt with shelves of books visible behind his head. A short biography said he'd written a dozen books since starting as a junior reporter in the 1980s and still lived in Great Yarmouth.

Great Yarmouth: that wasn't far away at all. Just an hour at most, unless he'd moved away in the intervening years.

Susan opened her laptop, an idea slowly taking shape. She typed his name into Facebook and saw the same photograph appear at the top of the list of people with the same or similar names. She clicked on it and found a basic profile that hadn't been updated in nearly two years. There was, however, an email address. She opened Gmail and began to compose a message, thinking the chances of his replying to her were slim.

But if she didn't try now, she knew, she would probably never try again. She hoped he might be able to give her his hopefully objective opinion on the EVP's.

Dear Mr Summerfield, she wrote.

My name is Susan MacDonald. I'm a senior researcher in advanced physics under contract to Ashford Innovations at the new research centre based in

Ashford Hall, Wardenby...

She paused, and decided she needed some *bona fides* to prove she wasn't some random nutter. She added her LinkedIn address at the top, along with a link to one of her published papers.

I hope this doesn't sound strange, she continued, *but I came across your book and I'd like to ask you some questions about the history of Ashford Hall and some of the observed phenomena there.*

She hesitated. Did that make her sound reasonable enough? Even using a phrase like *observed phenomena* sounded, given the context, like the kind of thing a person might say before trying to persuade you they'd invented a perpetual-motion machine, or had a radio that could talk to God.

But then again, this *was* a man who'd written a whole book about EVP's and séances. *What do you have to lose?*

Everything, she thought. *My reputation. My career.*

She laughed to herself and continued writing: *If it might be possible to speak to you, even for a few minutes, on the telephone or otherwise, I'd greatly appreciate it.*

Yours, Dr. Susan MacDonald, Ashford Hall Research Centre, Wardenby.

That should do it, she thought, pressing send.

Thursday July 9th 2020

When she checked her email the next morning, she found a reply had arrived from Summerfield sooner than she'd expected. It had been nearly midnight when she'd sent her email, so Summerfield must still have been up at that time. Metka, however, still hadn't returned her call.

Dear Miss MacDonald,

It makes a delightful change to receive an email from someone who doesn't urgently want to discuss my aura, although in all honesty I haven't had a single letter or query about Ashford Hall in very nearly five years.

If you'll pardon my indiscretion, I did very quickly look you up online, and judging by what I see and what little I understand I think I'm safe in assuming at least for the moment that you're sane. However, do be aware I keep a baseball bat within reach at all times.

If you're working at Ashford Hall, I'd very much like to talk to you.

He'd left his telephone number. Susan finished her coffee and toast and called it. He picked up after six rings.

'Mr Summerfield?' she said. 'I'm Doctor MacDonald.'

'Delighted to make your acquaintance.' His voice sounded dry and gravelly. 'I am to understand you're familiar with Ashford Hall?'

'Yes. It's been refurbished as a –'

'Some kind of *research* centre, yes.' She sensed caution in his tone. 'Does that mean you, ah... work for Christian Ashford?'

'I'm under contract to carry out a research project in Ashford Hall that's funded by his company. I don't think I work "for" him in the sense you mean. I'm speaking to you in my own private capacity. It's got nothing to do with him.'

'I see. So tell me, have you *heard* something, Miss MacDonald? Is that why you wrote me so late at night?'

'I consider myself a very rational person, Mr Summerfield. But...'

She heard him sigh down the line, his words crackling faintly with static. 'I'll tell you what, Doctor MacDonald. I've rarely if ever had the chance to speak to someone scientifically qualified on the matter of Ashford Hall without being dismissed outright as a charlatan. Neither do I get many visitors where I am who aren't trying to sell me some variety of voodoo nonsense. If you should care to visit, I'll give you the benefit of my company for a few hours, along with the benefit of my doubt, and I'll tell you more about Ashford Hall than you probably ever wanted to know.'

Susan passed through the outskirts of Great Yarmouth at midday that same day, her phone's GPS guiding her to a rambling cottage located behind tall hawthorn hedges. She pulled onto a short gravel driveway and saw Summerfield standing in the doorway of his house, his hands pushed deep into the pockets of well-worn slacks.

He was clearly a few decades older than the photograph, with a prominent belly and hair that had thinned on top. He wore a tatty jumper over a peach shirt, a pair of crumbling slippers on his stockinged feet. He raised a hand in greeting as she got out of her car, then guided her inside a living room dominated by numerous mismatched bookshelves stacked horizontally with hundreds of books. Typewritten sheets were haphazardly piled on a coffee table, while an antique-looking desk faced towards a four-paned window with what would have been a clear view of the English Channel were it not for the large iMac sitting on it.

'Sorry,' he said, picking up some books and notepads that had been discarded on his sofa. 'Research.'

'You're still writing?'

He glanced at her and smiled. 'You assumed I'd retired by now.'

'Sorry.' Her face warmed. 'I shouldn't have assumed...'

'Writers can't afford to retire,' he told her. 'And I have more debts than most.' He motioned to her to take a seat and she perched on the sofa while he pulled over the office chair before his desk. 'Ghost-writing mostly, these days – you won't see my name on most of the books I write. Appropriate, though, isn't it?'

She regarded him with confusion. 'I'm sorry?'

'*Ghost* writing.' He chuckled to himself. 'Never mind.'

'I nearly turned around a couple of times on my way here,' she admitted. 'I find it hard to talk about these things.'

'The supernatural?'

She returned a smile that was half-grimace. 'Trying to think of it in rational terms helps, but...'

'"The supernatural is the natural not yet understood",' said Summerfield. 'Or at least that's the quote I remember. Does that help any?'

'A little.' She brushed her hands down the thighs of her jeans. 'In your book, you described people hearing voices in Ashford Hall.'

'EVP's.' He nodded as if he'd won an argument. 'That's what brought you here?'

She nodded. 'Christian Ashford is funding my research project. I wasn't even aware of the building's history until Ashford hired parapsychologists to investigate something going on there.'

Summerfield nodded. 'I heard.'

'You did?'

'The Fortean Times asked me if I'd like to write an article about it, but I declined.'

'The Fortean what?'

He waved a hand as if to suggest it didn't matter. 'So what happened, exactly? Did you hear or see something out of the ordinary?'

'Not at first,' she replied. 'This is difficult for me to talk about, because I've started to wonder if there's some connection between the EVP's and my research.'

'Which is?'

'That's the difficult part,' she explained. 'I can't tell you anything in any real detail. I signed a non-disclosure agreement that means

Christian Ashford could sue me just for speaking to you about it in any capacity.'

Summerfield's expression soured. 'That does sound like the Ashford I know.'

'You've met him?'

'Personally? No. But I've dealt with him.' He nodded to her. 'Do continue, please.'

'I want to know what you think of the EVP's,' she said, 'if you think they're real or fake. I badly need an outside opinion, and you're the only person I can find right now who can give me one. I read your book, and it gave me the feeling you didn't believe in them.'

'I was trying to maintain an objective balance,' he replied, 'which is why I never presented any firm conclusions. I did hear something in those ruins, if that's what you mean, but as to their origin or nature, I remain undecided.' He shifted in his seat. 'I visited Ashford Hall three times in the company of people who invited me there. We spent one night in the room where Clara Ward died. I work hard to maintain my scepticism, but sometimes in the face of sheer evidence it can be hard to do so.'

'You wrote in your book about it.'

'Then you already know that the moment I heard something out of the ordinary, I left the room and searched the nearby ruins in case someone was hiding there.'

'But you didn't find anything or anyone.'

He shook his head. 'What I *didn't* write,' he emphasised, 'for the sake of my journalistic integrity, was how utterly terrifying the whole experience was.' He leaned forward in his chair, and fixed her with his gaze, his expression suddenly hard and flat. 'Now tell me, were you telling the truth when you said Ashford doesn't know you're here?'

She blinked at him in surprise. 'No, he doesn't. I told you I'd be in trouble if he knew.' She frowned. 'You don't actually think I'm *spying* on you, do you?'

'He came very close to ruining me, Miss MacDonald. That makes me a little uncomfortable about answering questions for *anyone* associated with him. It's also why I turned down the Fortean

Times – the last thing I want to do is attract his attention. If I publish one single word about either him or Ashford Hall, his legal firm will come down on me like the proverbial ton of bricks.'

She stared at him, astonished. 'I had no idea. I'd swear on a stack of Bibles or anything else you like I'm here purely out of my own interest.'

He glared at her for a few moments more, then appeared to relax again. 'Very well,' he said, his voice softer now. 'Then I have a proposal. In return for answering your questions, you tell me the exact nature of your enquiries, and screw the NDA. In return, we'll agree we never met or talked about any of this. Quid pro quo.'

'I can't do that. I told you, he'd sue me as well.'

Summerfield sighed and stood. 'Then I'd like to thank you for your visit, but I'm afraid it's over.' He went to stand by the living-room door and extended a hand towards the hallway.

She sat there, hands screwed up in her lap, and listened to the clamour of voices in her head urging her to leave. 'Fine,' she said at last, collapsing back against the sofa. 'Fact is,' she muttered, 'I don't have much to lose at this point.'

He regarded her for a moment, then nodded and stepped over to a drinks cabinet near his desk, taking out a bottle of whisky and a pair of glasses. 'A little of this might help bolster your clearly flagging spirits,' he said, pouring her a glass and handing it over before making one for himself. 'In fairness, the chances are excellent I won't understand half of anything you tell me about your work.'

'You might be right,' she allowed. 'But if we're going to do this, why don't you go first – why *did* Ashford cause you so much trouble?'

'Well,' he said, 'I may have implied in my book that his alibi was less than bulletproof.'

She nodded. 'Someone saw him riding around on his motorbike.'

'No,' Summerfield corrected her, '*someone* wearing all-concealing leathers and a helmet was seen riding around on a motorbike the same *model and colour* as Ashford's.'

'But it could have been anyone. That's how I read it anyway.'

'I had a very good lawyer who argued that exact same point,

Miss MacDonald, but, while Ashford's pockets are deep, mine are not.'

'So,' she asked, '*was* he in Wardenby when Clara Ward died?'

Summerfield's manner became cagey. 'Your turn,' he said. 'Maxim Bernard is highly regarded in his field, even by those who clump him together with the table-knockers. Why not go to him?'

'I know one of his assistants. I've spoken to her about this. But you were at Ashford Hall decades before they were, and clearly you're the expert on the subject.'

'And how do the EVP's relate to your work?'

'I'm building a... a kind of radio,' she explained. 'A highly experimental one that involves sending information back in time.'

He stared at her. 'What, a bloody time machine?'

She was starting to get tired of people calling it a time machine. 'Not exactly. It has to do with quantum mechanics —'

He put out a hand to stop her. 'Spare me the details. What does this have to do with ghostly recordings?'

'I don't know that it has *anything* to do with them,' she replied. 'But I heard an EVP that implies our machine somehow caught a random piece of conversation from inside the laboratory where it's kept and, in some way I don't understand, sent it backwards in time.'

'To where?'

'To Ashford Hall, before it was rebuilt.'

Summerfield's expression became thunderstruck. 'Am I to understand you think EVP's are actually messages from the *future*?'

'Well, from the present,' she corrected him. 'But that obviously doesn't account for all of them,' she added, thinking of that voice whispering to her in the room where Clara had died. 'Just the ones from the Halls.' *And maybe not all of those either*, she reminded herself, taking a drink of the whisky. She felt it burn away some of the chill in her belly.

'What led you to this conclusion?' he asked, clearly fascinated.

'The EVP I heard directly referenced the experiments I've been carrying out.'

He looked thoughtful. 'I suppose a physics experiment might make for a more rational explanation than the restless dead.'

She nodded. 'To be honest, I came here hoping you'd tell me

the EVP's are a load of rubbish.' She eyed him carefully. 'But that's not the feeling I get from you.'

'Well, you said yourself that you could only account for some EVP's. What about the rest?'

'That's where it gets really weird,' she said. 'It's certainly possible, hypothetically speaking, that some of the EVP's recorded in the vicinity of the Halls could be snatches of conversation somehow transmitted into the past. They're just information – they're not alive, so there's no way for them to directly interact with anyone.' Summerfield nodded. 'But the other day, someone – or some*thing* – seemed to speak directly to me.'

'What did it say?'

'It was saying my name. And then it said *He'll kill me.*' She shuddered, wishing she had an excuse to ask for another whisky. 'Over and over again.'

'Where exactly did you hear this?'

'Maxim Bernard had miked up the room where Clara Ward died. I happened to go in there without being aware of its history or even that the place was supposed to be haunted.'

Summerfield studied his own whisky for several seconds before speaking. 'When, exactly?'

'Last Friday. I... thought I heard a voice behind me when I was in the room, but when I turned around there was no one there. I heard nothing else at the time.' She put her whisky glass down carefully on the edge of the coffee table. 'Then Metka – that's one of Bernard's assistants – played me back what their mikes had picked up in the room. My name, and the words *Susan, he'll kill me* were buried deep in the static. I just about ran from the building when I heard it coming out of the speakers.'

'I'm not surprised. Would you like to hear something equally scary, Miss MacDonald?'

She laughed weakly. 'Not really, no.'

'I've heard the name Susan before,' he told her. 'You're in more than one of the EVP's. Do the words "beauty and the beast" mean anything to you?'

He must have seen something in her face, for he nodded with apparent satisfaction before she could formulate an answer.

She picked up her glass and drained the last of her whisky. 'Metka – Bernard's assistant – played me a recording with that phrase in it, along with my name.'

'Does the phrase "beauty and the beast" have some special significance to you?'

She nodded. 'Very much so, yes.'

'I see.' He swivelled in his chair to face his computer. He touched the mouse and the screen came to life. 'Before we speak any further, I'd like to play you something.'

Oh God. 'Is it another EVP?' she asked, knowing with dreadful certainty that it must be.

He nodded. 'This won't take a moment.'

She put down the empty glass and gripped her knees. Static filled the living-room, Summerfield slowly increasing the volume much as Metka had, until she could feel a low rumble transmit itself through the sofa's springs.

Before long she could just about make out a voice, tremulous but clearly feminine, and surprisingly clear for all the static. Each statement sounded like a whisper, and at times she looked over at Summerfield, thinking it was over, just for the voice to return again.

Susan
Ask Susan
The bracelet
I put it in his hand
You don't know how much it took
It's all his fault
I didn't know about beauty and the beast
Ask Susan
She'll come looking for you, David
The bracelet is all I had of me.

It was too much. She caught sight of Summerfield's shocked expression as she darted out of the living-room, just making it to the front door before yanking it open and vomiting onto a rose bush situated beneath a window. He heard him come hurrying after her, and felt something soft pressed into her hand.

'Dear God,' he said. 'I was worried it might unnerve you, but I never thought...!'

She took the napkin from him and pressed it against her mouth with shaking hands. 'I'm sorry,' she whispered. 'I don't know what happened.'

'I frightened the daylights out of you, is what happened,' said Summerfield. He touched one hand gently to her shoulder. 'I'm so very sorry. Please, come back in, at least so we can finish.'

She regarded him with alarm. 'There's more?'

'Of the recording?' He shook his head. 'No, you'll be glad to know. Here. Allow yourself to clean up a little.'

He guided her through to his toilet, where she washed her face and hands and looked at her pale skin before going back to join him in his living-room.

'I'd give you another whisky,' he said, 'but I know you have to drive back.'

'That's perfectly fine.' She lowered herself carefully back onto the sofa.

'Now you understand why I was so keen to meet you,' said Summerfield. 'That damn voice has – if you'll pardon the expression – haunted me for years. Then out of nowhere I get a phone call from a woman named Susan, who's working at Ashford Hall, which was still just a ruin until a year ago, wanting to know about the EVPs. So naturally...'

'I understand. Look, my research involves two communications devices, one here and one in California, codenamed Beauty and Beast. The Beast lives in Ashford Hall. It's a quantum communications array of a highly experimental nature.'

He stared at her with hungry fascination. 'I was present when that recording I just played you was made. You can imagine how I reacted when it was played back to me and I heard my own name.'

'The bracelet,' she said, standing suddenly. *It mentioned the bracelet.*

Summerfield blinked at her in surprise. 'It means something to you?'

She ran back out to her car without any further explanation, carefully avoiding looking at the rose bush on the way out and back again. She'd left the bracelet sitting on the dash after her encounter with the librarian. She brought it back in and gave it to Summerfield, who stared down at it in his hand.

'What is this?' he asked.

'A bracelet. I found it in the room where Clara died.'

'My God,' he said quietly.

'It's as real as Beauty and Beast,' she told him.

He chuckled quietly. 'My God,' he said again. 'My hands are shaking.'

'I heard workmen making a racket – or what I *thought* was workmen, but when I went to look there was no one there. I had no idea who Clara Ward was at the time or what had happened to her. The floorboards had been pulled up, and my shoe fell between the joists. I found the bracelet stuck between them, out of sight.'

Summerfield looked up from where he'd been turning the bracelet this way and that in his hands. 'Who else has seen this?'

'No one.'

He peered more closely at it, holding it up to the light. 'There's something written here...'

'"CA & CW",' she told him.

'So it does,' he muttered, and lowered it again. 'Good Lord – it must have been down there all this time.'

'I thought perhaps CA *might* stand for Christian Ashford, and CW for Clara Ward.'

'Or Claire,' he said, looking over at her.

Susan blinked, sensing that she'd missed something. 'Claire?'

'The sisters do have the same initials, Miss MacDonald.'

Susan put her hand to her mouth. 'Wasn't there something in your book about Ashford being involved with both of them?'

'There were certainly rumours,' he said, passing the bracelet back over. 'I heard them from some of the same people who told me they'd seen him on his motorbike, riding away from Ashford Hall on the night in question.'

'Then... Why didn't they speak up about it?'

Summerfield's expression was grim. 'Christian Ashford was a young man with prospects, Doctor MacDonald, sitting on a trust fund worth millions. Enough to buy their silence.'

'Then... You think he had something to do with Clara's death?'

Summerfield returned her a tight smile, as if to indicate that was the most he was prepared to say on that subject.

'All right,' she said. 'So what happened to *Claire* Ward? I don't recall you mentioning her much after the séance.'

'She still lives near Wardenby. Last I heard, she worked in the library.'

Shit. She'd forgotten about the librarian. 'There's something I need to tell you...' She quickly summarised the events in Wardenby's library.

He nodded once she'd finished. 'Perhaps,' he suggested, 'you should go to her and *ask* if the inscription refers to her, or her sister.'

Susan opened her mouth to respond, then hesitated. Summerfield's eyebrows drew close together as he waited for her to respond.

'You don't want to, do you?' he said at last. 'Why not?'

She didn't answer. Summerfield shifted in his chair, crossing one leg over the other. 'Perhaps *I* should go and ask her,' he said. 'Or even go to the police with it. That bracelet could be the most significant development in a case that's been closed for over thirty years.'

'No,' she said, holding the bracelet tight in her lap. 'Please. I – I need time to verify whether or not there's some clear, causal link between the EVP's and the quantum arrays. If there is, it could be one of the most important scientific discoveries in decades. But if there's any kind of investigation, I have no way of knowing what might happen to Ashford Hall or my experiment.' She had visions of police tape blocking the building entrance.

'Except Claire Ward already knows about the bracelet,' Summerfield reminded her. 'For all we know, she's already talked to the police about it. And then where does that leave you?'

'You said yourself the case has been closed for years. I only need a few more days to run some more tests, then I'll hand the damn thing in myself. Besides, it might have lain there forever if I hadn't stumbled across it when I did.'

'Then I suppose,' said Summerfield, standing now, 'that the decision rests with you. I can't say I envy you, Miss MacDonald.' She could see from his expression that he didn't approve of what she was doing.

'Thank you for speaking to me,' she said, standing as well. 'And thank you for playing me that recording.'

'Thank *you*,' he said, extending a hand, 'for resolving a mystery that's been stuck with me for years. I want very much to know how things work out. If you could keep in touch, I would very much appreciate it.'

'Of course.' She walked to the front door. 'Will you promise me you won't say anything to anyone about the bracelet?'

He nodded. 'You have my word. But if too much time passes, expect to get a reminder from me. You can't hold on to it forever.'

'Of course.' She dug her hand into her pocket and searched for her keys. A new idea was forming in her mind. 'I understand that.'

Summerfield pulled the door open. 'One last word of advice before you go. Secrets have a habit of coming up behind you and stabbing you in the back when you least expect it.'

By the time she had guided her car through the centre of Great Yarmouth, the idea that had been forming in her head coalesced and grew. When she stopped to check her messages and get some lunch, she saw that Metka had finally replied. Susan called her straight back and explained what she had in mind, then got onto the motorway and drove to Wardenby as fast as she could go without getting herself arrested.

Susan paused before getting out of the car at Ashford Hall. She had put the bracelet back on top of the dash, and she stared at it, thinking of all the things Summerfield had said. She picked it up and pushed it into a pocket, then grabbed her rucksack along with a plastic bag full of newspapers she'd picked up after lunch.

She found Metka waiting for her at the reception desk – unmanned, of course, both Pat and Dan having now quit.

'You have them all?' Susan asked her.

Metka patted a laptop bag slung over one shoulder. 'Complete archives of Arthur Melville,' she replied. 'Many more than are available to the public, along with transcripts of each.' She looked puzzled. 'I'm not sure I completely understand what it is you have in mind.'

'Doing is better than explaining,' said Susan, leading her up the steps to the upper floor. 'Just to be clear – how many EVP recordings are there altogether from Ashford Hall?'

'Almost one hundred and fifty,' Metka replied.

Susan's steps nearly faltered in her astonishment. 'That many? I had no idea.'

'There is a reason why Ashford Hall is so infamous,' Metka reminded her.

'The more the merrier, I guess,' said Susan as she unlocked the door of her laboratory. Neither Andrew nor Rajam were there – they'd have the place to themselves, as she'd hoped. 'Did you bring the camera?'

Metka nodded. She opened her bag and pulled out first a Dell laptop and then a small handheld video camera, placing them side by side on a table.

'Excellent,' said Susan, placing the bag full of newspapers and her rucksack next to each other on her desk. She took out the bracelet as well, and put it on top of a stack of journals. 'I had a conversation this morning with a man named David Summerfield.'

Metka nodded, surprise registering on her face. 'The man who wrote the book about Ashford Hall?'

Susan supposed it was natural Metka would have known about it. 'I read it the other day. Once I realised he didn't live that far from here, I got in touch with him. After the things you told me, I thought perhaps he could answer some questions for me.'

Metka's gaze was respectful. 'We wanted to consult with him for the case, but Ashford refused us permission to contact him. I'm beginning to think we should have had you working for *us*.'

That Ashford had refused them permission to meet with the man who'd linked him with an infamous murder didn't surprise Susan in the least. 'I got to thinking about what you said about a link between the recordings and my experiment. I'm willing to admit at least the possibility a link exists. But that doesn't mean a thing without experimental proof.'

'Then how do you prove it?'

Susan patted the stack of newspapers with one hand. 'With these.' She rifled around inside a drawer until she found a pair of scissors and passed them to Metka, who stared down at them in confusion. 'What we're going to do is very simple,' Susan explained. 'We're going to select several random pages from each of these newspapers, which are all this morning's editions, and then we're going to slice those pages up into random strings of text. Just short snippets no more than a few words long should be sufficient.'

'How many?' asked Metka, looking dubious.

'For the sake of randomness, I think a few hundred should do.'

Metka gazed at the stack of newspapers. 'That's going to take a long time.'

'I think we can get it done in just an hour or two at the most.' Susan bent at the knees and picked up a wastebasket, emptying the contents onto the floor before placing the basket on another desk. 'Once we're done, we'll chuck all of them in here and shake it until they're all mixed up. Then we'll take turns selecting fragments at random, sight unseen, and put them together to form nonsense statements.' She nodded at the door beyond which lay the Beast. 'Then we're going to run a test.'

'I think I see,' said Metka, glancing from the wastebasket to the newspapers and then towards the Beast, behind its door. 'You want to try and make your own EVP's. Is that it?'

Susan grinned widely. 'Nail on the head.' She checked the kettle was full and switched it on. They were going to need coffee to fuel them through the rest of the day.

'You get started with the scissors, and I'll get Beast operational in the meantime,' said Susan. 'Then I'll find another pair of scissors and get to work slicing up bits of paper as well.'

'And then?'

'And then,' said Susan, 'we're going to read out our nonsense statements. I figure we should do it right here, or in the room where the array is.'

'You think it makes a difference where we are when we read them out?'

'I have no idea,' Susan admitted. 'I thought about the room where Clara Ward died, but if the Beast is involved, I might as well assume proximity to it counts. Logic, or at least the prevailing evidence, dictates we need to be somewhere inside Ashford Hall for this to work.'

Not, she thought to herself, that there was any way in Hell she was ever going to enter that room of whispers and bracelets if she could humanly avoid it.

'Lastly,' she added, placing a hand on Metka's computer, 'and only after we've read them out, we'll see if there are any matches with any of the previously recorded EVP's.'

Metka laughed. 'Idea is brilliant,' she said. 'But no one will believe you had not first listened to the EVPs, then constructed appropriate statements to match them.'

Susan nodded sharply. 'You're absolutely correct. But think of this experiment as a proof of concept. I'm not expecting it to be absolutely rigorous – right now, the only people I'm trying to prove this to are you and me.' She picked a copy of the Daily Mail from the stack and started to separate out its pages. 'And keep in mind that I'm not really making up the nonsense statements – they're all from newspapers published today, so there's every reason to think any EVP's we create today will contain information found *only* in today's newspapers.' She studied the parapsychologist. 'So – are you in? Because if this works, you're going to be telling your grandchildren about the day you won half a Nobel prize.'

Metka lifted a copy of the Telegraph from the stack, then paused, regarding Susan with a serious expression. 'Is there not a risk that sending messages back in time breaks all kinds of laws regarding causality?'

'Yes,' Susan agreed, tearing sheets in half, 'that *is* something I've thought about.' Indeed, that was precisely why she had decided to transmit random information, rather than anything too specific such as the name of a recent US President or the fall of the Twin Towers. 'But until now, all we've had is theory and zero experimental proof of what does happen, if anything.' She handed the pages to Metka, then powered up Rajam's workstation. 'The only thing causality tells us is that if something can't happen, it won't happen. So let's see what *does* happen, shall we?'

In the end, it didn't take much more than an hour and a half to generate sufficient newspaper cuttings for Susan to feel they had enough randomised fragments for their purposes. They pushed them all into the wastebasket, then carried it next door to the Beast. After that, Susan went back through to Rajam's workstation and got to work programming the array.

'Okay,' she called through once everything was ready, 'fetch the camera and we'll get started.'

Susan smoothed her hair down, then turned to face Metka, who had switched on the camera and held it focused on her. There were a couple of false starts while Metka reminded herself how the machine operated, and Susan kept tripping over her own words, but soon enough she was able to quickly explain, for the sake of posterity, the nature of the experiment they were about to undertake.

Susan made a satisfied grunt when Metka tapped a button on the side of the camera. 'It's a start, anyway.'

'Whoever picks the cuttings out of the box should wear a blindfold,' Metka suggested.

'That's a great idea,' said Susan, sounding pleased. 'What can we use?'

'I have a bandana,' said Metka, fishing one out of a pocket. She shrugged. 'Better than nothing.'

Metka agreed to pick out the fragments while Susan read them out loud. They set the camera on a portable tripod Metka had fetched from the West Wing in one corner of the Beast's laboratory. Susan, in view of the lens, arranged the bandana carefully over Metka's eyes while she sat on a chair next to the Beast's table.

'I can still see through it a little,' said Metka.

'Cover your eyes with one hand as well if you want to,' Susan suggested. 'Remember, this is about proof of concept more than anything. If it works, we'll run the experiment again, preferably with other people involved, and see if the same thing happens.'

Metka nodded, and Susan placed the wastebasket carefully on the floor between Metka's legs where she could easily reach down with one hand. She even went so far as to spread a piece of cloth over the top of the wastebasket. For one moment, she had a sudden mental flash of herself as a magician's assistant, waiting to pull a rabbit out of an impossible hat.

'All right,' said Susan, leaning over to peer through the lens, her heart and lungs heavy in her chest, 'start picking them out.'

Metka reached under the cloth with one hand pressing the bandana against her eyes, and lifted out the first scrap of paper. Susan left the camera and took the scrap of paper from Metka, placing it on another piece of cloth she'd spread on the edge of the table. It read: *"don't burn the"*.

The next scraps pulled out of the wastebasket read: *"relatively, official announcement, said today"* and *"denied everything"*.

Metka continued, and Susan started a second line with the next group of scraps. Before long they had a good sixty or seventy words arranged into a half-dozen nonsensical-sounding statements – as close to truly random as Susan was able to get under the circumstances.

'Now what?' asked Metka, pulling the bandana off.

Susan took out her phone and pulled up the camera function before taking a snap of the words arranged on the cloth. She next mailed the picture to Metka. Metka's phone chimed in response.

'We'll take turns reading the lines to each other,' said Susan. 'Once we're done – and *only* after we're done – we're going to open up your laptop and see if there are any matches between our randomised statements and Melville's EVPs.'

The whole thing took just ten minutes, with Metka's camera recording everything. Then they went next door to the office, where Metka ran a search on her laptop with her phone propped up next to it so she could type some of their randomised statements into the search bar. Then she sat back and said something under her breath that was clearly in her native Polish.

'No one will ever believe us,' she said at last, looking around at Susan.

Her fingers moved once more across the keyboard. Static issued out of the laptop's speakers. Mixed in with the static, and just barely audible, was a voice that might have been Susan's own. *Trapped behind him – couldn't avert the catastrophe – prices are falling everywhere.*

Susan studied the picture on her own phone and felt something shift deep inside her bones. 'That's the fourteenth line,' she said, her voice a half-croak.

Oh my God, she thought. *This is huge. Really,* really *huge.*

And whether she liked it or not, she was going to have to tell Christian Ashford before he could pull the plug on her project.

Friday July 10th 2020

Andrew stared at her. 'Are you hung over?'

Susan nodded, and took another sip of black coffee. Last night she'd wound up back in the Grey Lady with Metka, where she'd received an impromptu lesson on Polish drinking games by way of a celebration. 'Yes, Andrew, I very much am.'

'I see.' Andrew placed his leather attaché case on a chair and perched on the edge of his desk. 'Now do you mind telling me just what's going on?'

She looked at him through bleary eyes. 'Did Ashford contact you yet?'

Andrew's face registered mild surprise. 'Yes, in fact he did. He woke me up at some ungodly hour to tell me he's midway across the Atlantic on a private jet. What's going on?' He glanced at the door beyond which lay the Beast, then looked back at her, eyes wide. 'Have we made some kind of progress?'

Susan nodded and put down her coffee. 'Were you aware Ashford was about to kick me off my own research project?'

Andrew's face reddened, and he said nothing.

'You *did* know.' She glowered at him. 'What did he offer you?'

'I...' He cleared his throat, trying and failing to mask his embarrassment. 'How did you find out?'

She said nothing. His eyes darted towards Rajam's workstation, and his shoulders sagged. 'Don't worry. I can guess.'

'Rajam's got nothing to do with this,' she warned him. 'Leave him out of it.'

'I didn't really have much choice in the matter,' he told her, his tone almost pleading. 'It was either keep running things here after you'd left, or I'd lose the chance to run my own research projects.'

'Christian Ashford is an absolute snake,' Susan snarled. 'But for the moment we're stuck with him because of those fucking contracts we signed.'

He peered at her curiously. 'You've spoken with a lawyer?'

'This morning. I could take Ashford to court, but it'd cost me everything and drag on forever. And in the meantime he'd get what he wanted while I was stuck on the outside with no career to speak of.'

'Yes.' Andrew's voice dropped a little. 'Yes, that sounds about right.' He cleared his throat. 'But at least that means you can understand why I –'

She shot him another look and he halted mid-sentence. 'Fine,' he said, and stood. 'I can leave, if you'd rather.'

'You can stay,' said Susan. *I'd rather keep you where I can see you.* 'And yes, we've had a breakthrough, in answer to your original question.'

'So... Beauty and the Beast are talking to each other?'

'No.' She saw the surprise in his face. 'We've discovered something entirely different has been going on the whole time.'

'Such as?'

She gazed wordlessly back at him.

He nodded. 'I see.'

'You haven't exactly given me reason to trust you,' she said. 'Mostly I'm just glad I didn't come back to find the locks had been changed.' She leaned back in her chair, arms folded.

'You said *we've* discovered something,' he said. 'Who's "we"? Do you mean Rajam?'

She thought about not telling him, but decided she wanted to see the look on his face. 'Actually, Metka has been an enormous help. Without her insight, I might have missed something very

84

important altogether.'

Andrew's face coloured. 'What did she do to help, exactly? Offer to realign your chakras?'

She felt the anger rise up inside her like something red and raw and alive. 'Maybe you had the right idea in the first place,' she said. 'Maybe you *should* leave.'

His face coloured, his lips thin and bloodless. 'Enjoy your time with Christian,' he snapped. 'You deserve each other.'

He turned, then, and stalked out the door. By the time she realised he'd left his case sitting by his desk, he was long gone.

She almost called after him, then thought better of it. *Screw him*, she thought, realising her coffee had turned cold. He could come back and collect it if he had the nerve to show his face again.

'I have to tell you, what you sent me, well – it just blew me away.' Ashford gazed up at the brightly lit exterior of Ashford Hall. 'Blew. Me. *Away.*'

She wondered if it was her imagination that made her sense a touch of uneasiness as he surveyed the building. Ashford certainly looked the part of the West Coast billionaire, his face lightly bearded and his receding hair cropped close against his skull. He wore the standard Silicon Valley tech guru uniform of faded jeans and tennis shoes, but his long, dark coat and silk scarf, she suspected, cost more than some people made in a year. His eyes peered out from behind a pair of steel-rimmed glasses, his hands pushed deep into coat pockets.

'It's nice to finally meet you in the flesh, Mr Ashford,' said Susan, shaking his hand. She'd gone home after her confrontation with Andrew and done her best to make herself presentable for Ashford's arrival that same evening, but as much as it pained her to admit it, even to herself, it would have been good to have Andrew there at that precise moment. He was much better at dealing with people face-to-face than she had ever been.

'Pleasure's all mine,' he said, putting a hand on her shoulder and nodding towards the entrance. 'I never thought I'd see this place again.'

'You weren't here when they finished rebuilding it?'

He laughed at that, a high, nervous chuckle. 'It isn't officially open yet – not *officially*, that is. We'll have a proper ceremony this autumn. I haven't seen this old place in the flesh since it was still just a pile of mouldy bricks.'

He turned to speak to the man who had driven him here in a limousine, and who, judging by his muscular build and unsmiling demeanour, doubled as a bodyguard. 'Wait in the main hall, Grigor. I won't be long.'

The man grunted, then followed them into the main hall. Inside, Ashford cast a puzzled glance at the unmanned reception desk. 'I see you're still having staffing problems.'

'They keep quitting,' said Susan, regarding him levelly. 'It's because of the voices.'

He chuckled nervously again. 'I guess I can't blame them, even if you've proven they're not ghosts. He looked at her. 'That's right, isn't it?'

She nodded. 'They're not ghosts.' She thought of other voices whispering from out of hissing static, but no way in Hell was she telling Ashford about *those*.

'But these EVP's or transmissions or whatever the hell you want to call them – they *are* all from the present? I mean, they're definitely not connected with anything else that might have happened here before now, am I right?'

'I'm quite certain all the EVP's associated with Ashford Hall are purely an epiphenomenon of our experimental process,' she lied. 'They go from our present and into the past – not the other way around.'

'Well,' he said, 'I'm relieved to hear you say that.'

She nodded. 'Perhaps we should go up, and I can show you the Beast.'

Rajam was waiting for them in the lab, which looked marginally tidier than it usually did. Susan went through the motions of introducing them, trying not to think too much about the job offer Ashford had already made to Rajam, and which they were all pointedly avoiding discussing.

'The array is through here,' she said, leading Ashford into the room next door.

Ashford made his way around the edge of the table supporting the array and peered down at the ranks of components and lasers his money had paid for. 'I've visited the other one in Berkeley, of course. I won't pretend to understand as much of it as I'd like.' He glanced at her. 'Isn't Andrew going to be here?'

'There wasn't time to let you know. He...' her voice trailed off, unable to find the right words.

'Quit?' Ashford asked mildly.

'He expressed some concerns over Metka's involvement because of her association with Professor Bernard. To be honest, expressing concerns is what he mostly does.'

Ashford nodded. 'Whether he's here or not, he's going to have to sign a new NDA. So will you, and anyone else with even the vaguest idea of what brought me here. That's to protect me and you and all of us.' He came back around the table and smiled. 'I'm so excited by this I can hardly tell you. It could mean so many of the things we think we knew about how the world works are wrong.'

She forced herself to smile back. 'Obviously we need to run repeats of the experiment. And as I said, it'll be necessary to bring in other people to run it for themselves and see if they can replicate our results. That's the most important thing of all.'

'Of course. Of course. I have faith in you, Susan. Always did.'

'Thank you,' she said. 'I... assume that means I'll continue to be in charge of my project?'

His smile didn't flicker, but for a moment she sensed the steely businessman behind the mask. 'I guarantee it,' he said. 'When will you be ready for another run? I'd like to see it with my own two eyes before we start talking about this to anyone else.'

'How about tomorrow evening? I'm sure you're tired after flying all the way here.'

His grin became more relaxed. 'Not so much as you might think. But I should get settled in, and there's other business I want to attend to while I'm back in the country.' He nodded towards the door. 'Can I assume Rajam is aware of the nature of the experiment?'

'He is.'

Rajam had taken it in his stride when she described the details of what she and Metka had done, even though she sensed he didn't really quite believe what she was telling him. But it was the least she owed him for warning her about Andrew and Ashford.

'I should talk to Metka as well,' he said. 'I assume she'll be joining us tomorrow?'

Susan nodded. 'She will be. She has to go down to London first, but she'll be back in the early evening.'

'Perfect timing,' he said, glancing at his watch. 'Shall we say seven tomorrow evening? That'll give me time to attend to some business of my own.'

'Of course.' She guided him to the door. 'I'll show you out.'

'No need,' he said. His skin glistened beneath the strip lights as he stepped out into the corridor. 'I'll show myself out.'

She watched him leave, the rapid drumming of his tennis shoes on the floorboards testament to the speed with which he exited the building. *You only need him for a few more days,* she reminded herself: enough time to run the same experiment for people who could verify what they were seeing, or at least vouch for her. Then she'd give the damn bracelet to the police and they could do with Ashford what the hell they liked.

Saturday July 11th 2020

'Hey!'

Susan turned to see a man in a suit hurry across the intersection towards her car where she was waiting for the lights to change. It took her a moment to recognise him as the estate agent from the café, Adam something-or-other. He knocked on her window, a wide grin plastered across his face.

She wound the window down. 'I think the light's about to go green, Adam.'

'Just wanted to check,' he said breathlessly. 'I heard on the grapevine that Christian Ashford's back in town.'

'How did you hear about that?'

'There's a picture of him at Heathrow in this morning's Sun. That, and someone saw his limousine driving back from Ashford Hall last night.'

She shrugged gamely. 'Then I guess the jig's up.'

'Thanks for confirming. I swear to God, I can practically feel the property values around here going up by the second. Best thing that ever happened to this town.' He slapped the open palm of his hand on the roof of her car in a rapid rhythm, and then he was off with a wave.

She shook her head and guided her car forward as the light changed. When she pulled up outside the Hall ten minutes later, a beaten-up old Mini was parked next to Rajam's car. She got out, locked her car and dropped her keys.

She heard a foot crunch on the gravel behind her when she bent to pick them up. She looked around, but there was no one there.

'Hello?' she called into the cool evening air.

Huh. No one there. She went on in, wondering if she'd only imagined it, or if it was yet another manifestation of whatever strange force had taken hold of the building. But that only ever happened inside the building, not outside.

There was still no security guard, of course. It was getting to the point she was surprised to find anyone sitting at the reception desk.

When she reached the lab, she found Ashford was already waiting there, sitting chatting with Rajam.

'Didn't your driver bring you?' she asked, surprised to see him. 'I didn't see the limousine –'

'I came in the Mini,' Ashford replied, then laughed. 'I gave Grigor the day off. Figured a rental would help me stay under the radar now the press know I'm in the country.'

'I guess we'd better get to it,' said Susan. She saw a stack of newspapers that Ashford must have bought, sitting on a chair. 'Rajam?'

'Everything's ready,' Rajam confirmed.

'I spoke with Andrew yesterday evening, by the way,' said Ashford. 'That man is far too stressed-out. He's on his way to an ulcer if he's not careful.'

'He is somewhat... fixed in his views,' Susan agreed.

Rajam let out a snigger, then caught himself. 'Sorry,' he muttered.

'He was very *polite* about it,' said Ashford, a hint of Englishness already creeping back into his accent. 'But it's not absolutely necessary for him to be here, is it?'

Susan shook her head. 'Myself and Rajam can handle all the technicalities of programming the array.' Her phone pinged and she pulled it out. 'Drat.'

'Problem?' asked Ashford.

'It's Metka. She's going to be late.'

Ashford looked concerned. 'How late?'

'She's on the train from London. She doesn't think she'll be much more than half an hour late, forty-five minutes at the most.'

'Well,' said Ashford, 'unless it's absolutely necessary for her to be present as well, maybe we should just go ahead with the three of us?'

The way he said it, it was clear he wanted no further delays.

'We *do* have to wait for her,' Susan said apologetically. 'She's got all the historical EVP recordings on her laptop, plus the transcriptions.' Susan tapped on her phone and sent a reply asking Metka to let her know the instant her train got moving again.

'If there's one thing I hate about this country,' Ashford muttered under his breath, 'it's the trains.'

Susan put her hands up. 'All right, here's what we'll do in the meantime. Myself and Rajam will get to work tearing up today's newspapers into strips the same way me and Metka did.' She nodded to the stack of newspapers. 'By the time she gets here, we'll be all set to go. You can witness the randomised statements we come up with.'

Susan talked Ashford through the process once again, and she and Rajam got busy with the newspapers. Ashford told them he had to make some calls and left the office with his phone.

'Oh yeah,' said Rajam suddenly after they'd been cutting and tearing up pieces of paper for about fifteen minutes. 'Someone came looking for you yesterday – a woman. I forgot to mention it.'

Susan looked up at him from where she sat next to her desk. Rajam sat crosslegged on the floor with a pair of scissors, dropping his article-fragments into the wastebasket sitting between them. 'When?'

'Yesterday afternoon, about two.'

After she'd spoken with Andrew, and before she'd met Ashford that same evening. 'Polish accent, short hair, that kind of thing?'

'The woman who works with Bernard and Angus?'

Rajam shook his head. 'No, it's no one I've seen before. I think it was a local woman, actually.'

Susan stopped working with her scissors and looked carefully at him. 'Who, exactly?'

'I have no idea. See, that's the weird thing. Far as I could tell, she'd just wandered in from outside.'

'And there was no one at reception, of course. She didn't give you her name?'

He shook his head. 'I asked, but she refused.'

Somewhere in the back of Susan's head alarm bells began to ring. 'Tell me what she looked like.'

'Mousy, with brown hair, a cardigan and jeans. I think I might have seen her around Wardenby.'

Oh dear God.

Susan turned to look for the bracelet where she'd left it on her desk, but it wasn't there. She stood and pushed her hands through the papers and journals scattered across the desk, but there was no sign of it.

'What is it?' asked Rajam, looking puzzled.

'I left something here,' she said. 'But I can't find it.' Rajam had just described Claire Ward. Could she possibly have seen the bracelet? It would have been so very easy for her to just snatch it up without Rajam even being aware.

It struck her, then, that Ashford had been gone for some time. And she could smell burning.

She went through to look at the Beast, afraid Rajam's repair work might have caused some component to go up in smoke, but it looked the same as ever. When she returned to the office, she found Rajam standing at the door leading into the corridor, looking either way and loudly sniffing at the air.

'I think there's smoke,' he said, pulling his head back in.

She made her way over and sniffed the air as well. When she looked out into the corridor in the direction of the grand staircase, she could see wisps of smoke drifting out of the South Wing corridor.

'Call the fire brigade,' she said tersely. 'The alarm should have gone off.'

'Sure.' He pulled out his phone and began dialling. 'I'll check that all the data's backed up as well.'

She nodded. 'Good idea. I need to go find Ashford and make sure he's okay. How long should those backups take?'

'Not long,' he said. 'Most of the data's stored offsite, but I don't usually backup the last twenty-four hours until the end of the day.'

'In that case,' she said, 'forget it. Just get yourself outside.'

He hesitated. 'Maybe *I* should go and look for –'

'No,' she said adamantly. 'You're *my* responsibility. Get yourself outside, now, until the fire crews get here.'

Rajam was about to say something when the operator picked up. He hurriedly explained what was happening and hung up. 'Should be here in twenty minutes,' he said.

Better than nothing. She had a terrible feeling whatever was happening was in some way her fault. She and Rajam hurried along the corridor to the top of the main staircase, where they stopped, hearing loud and angry voices shouting at each other from somewhere down the far end of the South Wing corridor. One of them was recognisably Ashford's, but it was impossible to see who he was with through the smoke drifting towards the stairs.

'Go check the West Wing,' said Susan. 'See if Bernard or your friend Angus are there and get them out if they are. And as soon as you've done that, get the hell outside.'

'But what about you?'

'I'll find Ashford.'

'But –'

'Rajam,' she snapped, 'just *go*.'

He nodded, his face pale, then hurried down the West Wing corridor. It occurred to Susan the reason the fire alarm hadn't gone off was that it probably hadn't even been wired up.

She pressed the sleeve of her shirt over her mouth and nose and started to make her way down the South Wing corridor, crouching to keep under the layer of smoke drifting along beneath the ceiling. The further she went, the more she could hear the crackling of flames. She came to a laboratory and saw that it was ablaze: the heat was so intense she had to run past it as quickly as she could.

Then she saw them: Ashford and Claire Ward, struggling with each other next to the South Wing balcony.

'You killed her!' Claire screamed. She was beating at Ashford's face and shoulders while he tried desperately to fend her off. 'You were here and you *killed* her and you –'

'For God's sake, you crazy bitch!' Ashford shouted. He managed to get hold of her arms and she struggled like a wildcat in his grasp.

'You *lied* to me!' she screamed. 'You –'

They had moved closer to the top of the stairs. Susan took a step forward, then cried out at a sudden rush of heat at her back. She spun around, hands up to shield her face, and saw a great gout of flames come pouring out of the laboratory behind her. The fire was spreading far more quickly than she would have believed possible.

Susan turned back in time to see Ashford strike Claire across the head with something she couldn't quite make out. Claire's body immediately went limp, and she fell backwards over the balcony and out of sight.

Susan heard a thump, and then silence.

Ashford turned towards Susan and started in such a way that it was obvious he hadn't realised anyone else was there – so focussed had he been on his argument with Claire. He was breathing hard, his chest rising and falling from exertion. For the first time Susan saw the hammer gripped in his hand, its handle dark with Claire's blood. Workmen's tools were still scattered next to a painter's ladder.

'It was an accident,' he shouted over the roar of the flames. His voice took on a pleading tone, as if trying to convince himself as much as her. 'An *accident.*'

The growing heat of the flames behind her forced Susan to move closer to Ashford. She couldn't take her eyes from the hammer gripped in his hand. If she could just get past him and make a run for it down the stairs, she could get to the doors leading into the gardens and make her escape.

'I know it was,' she said. 'I saw what happened. It was an accident.'

His eyes narrowed. 'You saw what happened?'

She realised she had made a mistake. She threw herself past him and down the steps, feeling his hand lunge out to try and grab her arm. She managed to yank it free, then hurried down the steps, seeing Claire lying sprawled on the floor below, her neck twisted at an odd angle. The bracelet lay near one of her hands.

Susan grabbed hold of the doors and yanked at them furiously, realising to her horror that they were locked. There was no way out. But then she remembered the corridor that ran directly beneath the grand staircase, connecting the main hall to the gardens. So all she needed to do was –

The world crashed down on top of her skull before she could as much as turn around.

She collapsed, boneless, next to Claire's body, although she did not lose consciousness. She tasted iron on her tongue, and when she tried to move, her limbs refused to respond. Claire's dead eyes stared back at her as if to say *I told you so*.

She felt hands lift her under her armpits, Ashford grunting with the effort. She tried feebly to resist, to shake him loose as he dragged her back up the steps to the upper balcony. Her head seemed filled with a distant booming, like the crash of surf on a faraway shore.

Once he'd hauled her all the way up, Ashford kept dragging her until they were in the room where he'd murdered Clara Ward. He dropped her like a heavy sack, and she saw the room was unchanged since she had last seen it. The smoke rasped in her lungs.

Only then did it come to her that Ashford was going to leave her there to die. He was hoping the flames would burn her body so badly the true cause of death would never be found.

He left, then, but she wasn't at all surprised when he reappeared some minutes later, dragging Claire's body after him. He was red-faced and winded, his clothes dirty and rumpled from ash and smoke.

He looked down at Susan, panting hard. 'I'm sorry, okay? Wrong place, wrong time. It sucks.' He stared down at Claire's body and shook his head. 'Man, if you'd only known her when she was younger.' He moved towards the door and raised a hand. 'I'll make sure you get full posthumous credit for anything that comes out of any future research.'

'Wait,' Susan managed to mumble.

'Sorry,' said Ashford. 'I –'

Somewhere behind Susan's head and out of her sight, a floorboard creaked. She heard a sigh of wind that might have been a whisper, and had the undeniable sense that there was someone else in the room with them.

Standing right behind Susan where she lay.

Whatever it was, Ashford was staring speechless at it, his eyes full of animal terror.

And then Metka appeared behind him at the doorway, a two-by-four gripped in both hands. She brought it around in a smooth arc so that it smacked Ashford hard across the back of his head. The billionaire investor's knees folded, and he crumbled to the floor without so much as a sound. Metka let the plank tumble to the floor, then knelt quickly by Susan's side.

'You're still alive?' she asked, studying Susan with deep concern.

Susan managed to mumble an affirmative.

'Rajam told me you were still somewhere in here,' she said, hoisting Susan over her shoulders in a fireman's carry. 'Thought you must be dead when I saw the flames. I heard everything Ashford said.'

Metka carried Susan all the way back down the rear stairway and out through the now-unlocked doors into the garden, swearing and grunting under her breath the whole time before depositing Susan on the grass.

'Did you see anything?' Susan finally managed to say, her words slurred. 'In that room. There was someone behind me.'

Metka stared at her with a curious expression. 'I saw nothing.'

She looked back at the Halls, now entirely ablaze. From somewhere far away, Susan heard the sound of approaching sirens.

One Year Later

When Metka saw Susan on the steps of the Old Bailey the following summer, she pulled her into a bear-hug. It was the first time they'd seen each other in months.

'You look so thin,' said Metka, standing back and giving Susan an up-and-down look. 'You are... getting around all right?'

She meant the walking-stick, of course. 'It's not so bad,' said Susan. She moved the stick to her other hand. 'I'm fine, really.'

Metka nodded. 'So you're still getting physical therapy?'

'And will be, for some time yet.'

Metka winced in sympathy. 'I read that article in the Guardian about Ashford. My God. Such a terrible man.'

As it turned out, Claire Ward had kept extensive diaries ever since her sister's murder. Most of them were filled with gibberish: Claire had fallen in with an occult society whose members sat listening to radio static in the hopes of hearing and transcribing the voices of undead spirits. It was, journalists had concluded, her desperate attempt to get in touch with her dead sister.

Susan had been a primary witness in the inquest, of course. When she'd told Claire she had found the bracelet beneath the floorboards, Claire had realised the only way it could have got there was if Christian had dropped it while struggling to kill Clara. That realisation had driven her to set a fire in Ashford Hall before confronting Ashford in the South Wing.

All of this, in turn, had led to a reinvestigation of Ashford's alibi, and several people, including a former MP for Wardenby and a senior clergyman, were facing fresh perjury charges. Ashford himself had died in the flames. The down-and-out jailed for Clara's murder, meanwhile, was expected to receive a posthumous pardon.

Susan glanced back up the steps. 'You attended the inquest?'

Metka nodded. 'I was watching from the public gallery. I only just got back from South America this weekend.'

The hesitancy in Metka's English had entirely disappeared, Susan noticed. 'I was beginning to wonder what had happened to you when I didn't hear from you for so long,' she said. 'Were you in Venezuela all this time?'

Metka nodded. Susan knew that she'd gone there with Professor Bernard and Angus as part of some ongoing investigation. 'We were in a rural part of the country with almost no cell coverage,' Metka explained, rooting around in a shoulder bag. 'It made it almost impossible at times to contact anyone in the outside world.' At last she pulled a hardback book out of the bag, then passed it over. 'Here,' said Metka. 'This is for you.'

Susan saw that it was the updated edition of Summerfield's book, with a smarter, more modern cover design. 'So it's out,' she said, taking it from Metka. She stood carefully with her stick tucked under one arm and turned the book over to see a much more recent picture of Summerfield on the back, looking as saturnine as she remembered him.

'You get mentioned several times,' Metka told her. 'You know, you're practically famous in some quarters.'

'Have you eaten any lunch?' Susan asked her.

'Not yet,' said Metka.

'This time,' said Susan, 'it's on me.' And she led the way down the steep concrete steps, leaning heavily on her stick.

Susan had her own questions to answer during the inquest, of course, but surprisingly few had focused on the fact of her having held on to the bracelet quite as long as she had. As Summerfield himself had pointed out, after all, the case had been closed for decades. There was no reason for Susan, a civilian, to suspect the bracelet might be connected to an abuse of justice. As far as the law was concerned, she had committed no crime or misdemeanour.

When she gave her evidence, she made no mention of whispering voices, or whatever it was that had so terrified Ashford in those last moments before Metka came to her rescue.

Ashford Industries had been taken over by its senior management team, and they had already changed the name of the company to put distance between themselves and their deceased founder.

Susan and Metka found a Wetherspoons that was remarkably quiet for the middle of London on a weekday afternoon. They picked at their fish and chips and Rogan Josh and talked about the things they'd done since they'd last seen each other.

'They really aren't letting you access your own experimental results?' Metka shook her head, scandalised, as their coffee arrived.

'No," said Susan. "In fairness, the data's their property, but that doesn't mean I have to like it.'

'But none of it would have existed without you!'

Susan chuckled weakly. 'Doesn't matter. The experiment didn't work.'

Metka looked confused. 'But the EVP's – that experiment we did? Surely, I thought...'

'Fundamentally unsound and subjective, unfortunately.'

'But it *worked*,' Metka insisted. 'I was there. We both were.'

Susan sipped her coffee. 'It doesn't count, unless you can reproduce the results. And no one can.'

Metka leaned towards her. 'Why not?'

'Think about it. How many major physics research centres are haunted in the way Ashford Hall was? None. The EVP's existed there for a long time before we turned up.'

Metka thought about it. 'I see your point. You would have to set up the experiment in some place that already had a reputation...' Her eyes lit up. 'Then why not do just that?'

'I heard from Bethany the company's new owners did exactly that with Beauty – set it up in some abandoned hospital, with a history of hauntings and ghostly voices.'

'And?'

Susan shrugged. 'They found zero correlations with historical EVP's.'

Metka sank back. 'But it seemed as if we really had something.'

'We did,' said Susan. She rescued a lone chip from her plate. 'I think there was something special about Ashford Hall – something that made it unique.' She nodded at the book lying on the table between them. 'You remember what happened at the séance?'

Metka thought for a moment. 'Claire was accused of somehow ruining the proceedings.'

'Specifically, they asked the spirit for its name, and instead of saying Clara, it said Claire.' Susan gave Metka a meaningful look. 'I think that the séance made contact with Claire's ghost.'

Metka let out a baffled chuckle. 'Now you're confusing me. Claire was present and alive at the séance. Living people cannot haunt buildings, Susan.'

'Look – we found evidence that we were able to send certain types of information into the past, right?' Metka nodded. 'So on that Saturday we were supposed to run the experiment with Ashford present, I'd already set the array in motion when he wandered off to make a call. All that was left for us to do was read out our randomised passages.' Susan leaned across the table. 'By some mechanism I still can't even begin to understand, that information – our voices – were already being sent back to apparently indeterminate points in Ashford Hall's past.' She stabbed her still-uneaten chip in Metka's direction. 'But who's to say only our voices could be sent back in time?'

'Then... What else?'

Susan smiled. 'How about the spirit of someone recently deceased?'

Metka's mouth opened, then closed again.

'What I'm saying,' continued Susan, 'is that Claire's undead spirit, her *essence*, it could be argued, constitutes a form of data. One that could be transmitted to an earlier point in time by whatever weird physics we'd somehow tapped into.'

Metka's eyes had become round. 'Then... You're suggesting *Claire* was haunting Ashford Hall for all those years, and not Clara?'

She stared past Susan at some indeterminate point, thinking it through. 'So – after Ashford had killed her, her spirit somehow found its way through the array and into the past?'

'It makes sense of what happened at the séance, doesn't it? There were multiple witnesses to what happened there, so what if the spirit they'd contacted was simply telling *the truth*? And that EVP you played me, of a woman's voice whispering to me so low I couldn't hear it. *Susan, he'll kill me*, over and over.'

The blood drained from Metka's face. 'My God. You think that was Claire trying to *warn* you?'

'Warn me that Christian Ashford was going to murder her, yes.'

'But... There are all those other EVPs we have on record. Are you saying she was responsible for all the rest of them?'

'Who knows?' Susan shrugged. 'After what happened, I'm willing to entertain just about any crazy idea.' She shrugged. 'Maybe some of them were echoes from parallel universes. The fact is, we'll never find out.'

Metka shivered visibly. 'You've been thinking about this a lot.'

Susan rolled her eyes. 'I've had little else to think about. I spent six months lying in a hospital bed trying to relearn how to walk. And research positions haven't exactly been landing at my feet in the meantime.'

'I'm sorry to hear that. So you haven't been working?'

Susan shook her head. 'I've got a teaching position starting in October. I can't really complain, but...It's not where I saw myself at this point in my life, put it that way.'

'I'm sorry.'

'No.' Susan shook her head emphatically. 'Don't be. It's my own fault, anyway.'

Metka studied her closely, then slowly began to shake her head. 'Susan, none of what happened is your fault. I don't see how you can possibly –'

'I wouldn't have wound up working for Ashford if I'd just kept my head down and stopped demanding credit; I'd have got to where I wanted to be eventually. And that bracelet...' She sighed. 'I hung on to it because I was afraid if Ashford really had something to do with Clara's murder, and the bracelet connected him to it, then it would risk my project.' She spread her hands, remembering how Summerfield had tried to warn her and how she had refused to listen. 'Do you see? I was thinking of myself, not those poor girls. If Claire hadn't seen the bracelet in the library, if I hadn't told her where I'd found it, she'd never have come to confront Ashford and they'd both still be alive.' She stopped herself, suddenly aware her voice had been rising. 'The way I see it, that makes me at least tangentially responsible.'

'You did what you had to do,' Metka insisted. 'You couldn't possibly have known what would happen.'

'No, I couldn't,' Susan agreed. 'But Claire's spirit knew. And all this time it was trying its damnedest to warn us about Ashford.'

'And we didn't listen.'

'No,' said Susan, slowly shaking her head. 'I'm afraid we didn't.'

Coda

'There you go,' said Adam Phillips, pushing the front door open and stepping to one side. 'Do you need any help with that step...?'

'I'm perfectly fine,' said Arthur Melville, placing the brass tip of his cane against the step and carefully levering himself across the threshold and into the narrow hallway of the house. Thin grey hair curled around the collar of his long dark coat, his mouth twisted up with just a suggestion of distaste.

Adam watched from the doorway as Melville reached for a light switch, flicking it back and forth to no effect.

'The electricity is still off,' Adam explained, his tone carefully apologetic. The old duffer seemed the type who appreciated a subservient attitude. 'It's been a year, after all.'

'Ah.' Melville nodded. 'Perhaps if you were to draw the curtains in some of the rooms, that might help?'

Adam stared into the shadowy hallway, and somehow found the courage to walk into the house, aware of the way the old man was looking at him. However much Melville's hand trembled where it gripped the cane, his eyes were sharp and unyielding in their focus.

Adam sniffed the air, mausoleum-cold and scented with dust and mould. He made his way into the living-room, drawing back the curtains and letting in thin afternoon light. Melville followed in his wake, studying the meagre furnishings with a disdainful eye. The light revealed cheap furniture not good for much outside of a scrapyard. Adam had developed a certain instinct when it came to the homes of the deceased, and he knew they would find no lost Rembrandt tucked under the bed or pushed to the back of a cupboard.

Melville turned to look at him. 'It's been empty since Miss Ward died, I presume.'

'It has.' Adam gestured around at the furniture. 'I have a firm I use for clearances. They can come around and get rid of all this old furniture even before we hand the keys over to you –'

'No,' Melville said abruptly. 'It was bad enough when the police were here.'

Adam blinked. 'I don't understand...?'

Melville pushed at a pile of Home & Gardens mouldering on a coffee table with the tip of his cane, and some of them slid off onto the floor. 'They took things,' he said with evident disgust, 'including Claire's diary. I only just managed to reacquire it, and it's been a year since she died. I don't want anyone else in here touching things that don't belong to them.'

Adam shivered, but not from the cold. The old man gave him the creeps. He'd heard a rumour Melville used to visit Claire Ward here in her house, and the assumption had been they were having some sort of affair. Yet there were other rumours, to do with Ashford Hall and some cult in Brighton.

'But surely, if you're moving in...?'

Melville smiled stiffly. 'I didn't buy this property to live in it, Mr Phillips.'

'I don't understand. Do you mean you intend to let the property out? That would require a different type of mortgage than the one you–'

'No tenants,' Melville said sharply. He took another glance around the bare, cold living-room. 'I intend to use it as a... meeting place.'

'A –' Adam caught himself before he could ask anything more. Who cared, really, *what* the old dingbat wanted with the place? It was hard enough selling a house associated with a grisly murder, so when Melville had appeared with an offer of just over half of what the property's market value had been prior to its owner going up in flames along with Ashford Hall, Adam had jumped at the chance to get rid of it.

A mobile phone rang, making Adam almost jump. Melville reached into the depths of his coat and withdrew a smartphone, placing it against his ear.

'If you would,' said Melville, catching Adam's eye and nodding at the door.

'Of course.' Adam stepped back into the hallway. It smelled terrible. A year without any heating meant the whole place was probably thick with mildew. He stepped into the kitchen, similarly untouched since its owner had left it for the last time. The walls of the old house were thick enough he couldn't hear Melville next door speaking to whoever it was on the phone. Even the garden outside the kitchen window seemed still and silent, as if anything living that crawled or swam or flew had chosen to abandon it.

He reached for an ancient transistor radio sitting on a counter and turned it on, finding the silence oppressive, but no matter how he turned the dial all he could hear was static, and the faint echoes of voices transmitted from far, far away. He thought he caught a trace of music, but no matter how he turned the dial he couldn't find it again.

He carried the radio over to the window and tried once more. After a moment he got something a little clearer, but it was just a man's voice, apparently crying out in pain.

Adam frowned, and listened more closely. *Help me*, he heard the voice say, and then again: *help me. Don't let them find me. Please. I'm so sorry. It was an accident. I didn't mean it to happen. Claire, please, it was an accident. Please don't. Please don't. Claire...*

He dropped the radio and it fell to the floor with a clatter before falling silent.

'Mr Phillips?'

Adam looked up suddenly to see Melville watching him from the door with a strangely knowing look. 'Perhaps,' he said, 'we should discuss when I can get the keys.'

'Of course.' Adam brushed trembling hands across his suit and tie, straightening it. 'If we step outside, I can call the office and arrange a pickup date.'

'After you,' said Melville with a bemused smile, as Adam made for the front garden with what under any other circumstances would have appeared to be unseemly haste.

About the Author

Gary Gibson is the author of ten novels, including *Stealing Light* (first in the four volume Shoal Sequence), and *Extinction Game*, and various short stories. A native of Glasgow, he currently lives in Taipei. He has a blog and website at: www.garygibson.net.

Selected Bibliography:

Angel Stations (2004)
Against Gravity (2005)

Shoal Sequence
1 Stealing Light (2007)
2 Nova War (2009)
3 Empire of Light (2010)
4 Marauder (2013)

The Final Days
1 Final Days (2011)
2 The Thousand Emperors (2012)

The Apocalypse Duology
1 Extinction Game (2014)
2 Survival Game (2016)

Cover art by Ben Baldwin

NewCon Press Novella Set 4: Strange Tales

Adam Roberts – The Lake Boy

Cynthia lives in a lakeside parish in Cumbria, where none suspect her blemished past. Then a ghostly scar-faced boy starts to appear and strange lights manifest over Blaswater. What of the astronomer Mr Sales, who comes to study the lights but disappears, presumed drowned, only to be found naked days later with a fanciful tale of being 'hopped' into the sky and held within a brass-walled room? What of married mother of two Eliza, who sets Cynthia's heart so aflutter?

Ricardo Pinto – Matryoshka

Lost in Venice in the aftermath of the war, Cherenkov just wants to put his head down somewhere and sleep, but her copper hair snares his eye. She leads him to Eborius, a baroque land lost in time, and takes him on a pilgrimage across Sargasso seas in search of the Old Man, who dwells on an island where time follows its own rules. Last of his kind, the Old Man is the only being alive who may hold the answers Cherenkov craves.

Hal Duncan – The Land of Somewhere Safe

The Land of Somewhere Safe: where things go when you think, "I must put this somewhere safe," and then can never find them again. The Scruffians: street waifs Fixed by the Stamp to provide immortal slave labour. But now they've nicked the Stamp and burned down the Institute that housed it, preventing any more of their number being exploited. Hounded by occultish Nazi spies and demons, they leave the Blitz behind in search of somewhere safe to stow it…

Lightning Source UK Ltd.
Milton Keynes UK
UKHW04f2302180918
329129UK00002B/366/P